MERCILESS

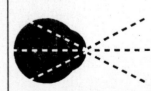

This Large Print Book carries the
Seal of Approval of N.A.V.H.

MERCILESS

DIANA PALMER

WHEELER PUBLISHING
A part of Gale, Cengage Learning

GALE
CENGAGE Learning·

Detroit • New York • San Francisco • New Haven, Conn • Waterville, Maine • London

GALE
CENGAGE Learning·

LIBRARY OF CONGRESS CATALOGING-IN-PUBLICATION DATA

Palmer, Diana.
    Merciless / by Diana Palmer. — Large print ed.
      p. cm. — (Wheeler Publishing large print hardcover)
    ISBN-13: 978-1-4104-3873-7
    ISBN-10: 1-4104-3873-2
    1. United States Federal Bureau of Investigation—Officials—Fiction.
2. Single mothers—Fiction 3. Large type books. I. Title.
PS3566.A513M4729 2011
813'.54—dc22   2011025468

Published in 2011 by arrangement with Harlequin Books S.A.

Printed in Mexico
2 3 4 5 6 7 15 14 13 12 11

To D.A. with much gratitude.

1

The attractive blonde sitting on the chair beside Jon Blackhawk's desk in the San Antonio FBI office was as irritating as most of the prospective brides his well-meaning mother threw at his head. He was impatient and half out of humor already, with testimony on an upcoming court case awaiting him. This woman's fascination with the latest trend in hairstyles was leading him to think of bars. And he never took a drink.

"See, mine was done by Mr. James at Sherigan's," she continued, indicating her haircut, which looked quite frankly as if someone had put her head in a blender. He bit his tongue trying not to make the comment out loud. "He could do wonders for you. That long hair is *so* retro!"

There was a perfunctory knock at the door and his administrative assistant, Joceline Perry, stuck her head in the door. "Excuse me, Mr. Blackhawk, but you're due in court in ten minutes."

He nodded, forcing himself not to dance on the desk with glee. It would have been totally out of character, but the past thirty minutes of fashion information had left him feeling brainless.

He got to his feet. "It was good to see you, Charlene. Please give my love to my mother when you see her."

"I'll be seeing her tonight, since we're going to the theater together. It's a production of that romantic comedy that Shakespeare wrote, in a modern setting," she enthused. "Your mother has three tickets to it," she added with a hopeful smile.

He cleared his throat and tried desperately to think of an excuse.

Joceline, her blue eyes twinkling, interjected, "There's that meeting with your informer tonight at seven," she lied.

"Oh. Oh, yes, thank you," he said, trying not to sound as relieved as he felt. "Another time, perhaps," he told Charlene.

She shrugged. "I suppose your job requires you to do things at odd times," she said. "You might think about another profession," she said with a thoughtful frown. "I mean, if you get married, you won't have time for these evening job-related thingies."

His black eyes glittered. "I have no plans

to marry."

She gave him an odd look. "Your mother said you were ready to start a family," she said blandly.

The glare darkened. "My mother has plans of her own. They are not mine," he added firmly.

Charlene gave him a charming smile and touched the sleeve of his gray suit jacket with a well-manicured hand. "Well, most men don't want to marry and have a family, until they realize how nice it is."

He didn't bend an inch.

Charlene sighed. "Rome wasn't built in a day," she ventured.

"It was, however, sacked by Charles V and his forces in one of the most violent attacks in military history," Joceline said with a sigh. "The Pope was forced to flee for his life." Her blue eyes went dreamy in their frame of short, straight black hair that just covered her small ears. "Charles V was the father-in-law of Mary Tudor, who was the sister of Elizabeth the First. Mary was in her thirties and Philip II was in his twenties when they married. It was a very strange match. But royalty in the sixteenth century was somewhat different in attitude." She smiled. "Do you study history?" she asked Charlene.

"Ugh," Charlene said, and shuddered

9

dramatically. "What a sick and horrible subject. Old dead people."

Joceline's eyebrows arched. "The past determines the future," she said. "For instance, did you know that in seventeenth-century America, women were accused of witchcraft and hanged for any sort of misbehavior?" She cocked her head. "That blouse you're wearing would have landed you in a river in Massachusetts in no time. You see, there was a common belief that only witches floated when thrown into bodies of water," she added helpfully. She smiled again.

Charlene gave her a blank look. "This is the latest fashion," she pointed out. She glared at Joceline's neat black skirt, small-heeled black shoes and blue button-up blouse. "You might have been jailed for having such awful fashion sense," she countered with contempt.

"No, no, they didn't jail people for that," Joceline replied smoothly. "They put them in stocks, but not for being conservatively dressed." She cocked her head again. "However, women who cheated on their husbands were branded with a large letter A."

Charlene cleared her throat and glared even more. "I am separated from my husband and we are in the process of a divorce."

"Really?" Joceline asked, all eyes. "Well,

isn't it lucky this is the twenty-first century?" she asked.

"I did not cheat on him!" Charlene raged.

Joceline's blue eyes were innocent. "I never insinuated such a thing!"

Charlene's face flushed. Beside her slender hips, against the expensive fabric of her slacks, her manicured hands were clenched. "The gentleman in question and I were merely having supper together after the theater! It was all lies!"

"I'm certain that it was," Joceline said with a bland smile.

Jon had been enjoying the repartee, but he quickly collected himself. "Ms. Perry, aren't you working on a case?" he asked deliberately.

She blinked. "A case, sir?" she asked.

"Follow-up interviews in my kidnapping court case?"

"The court case. Right." But she didn't leave.

Charlene was more irritated than ever. She grabbed her purse. "I see that it's an inconvenient time for us to talk," she told Jon. She went close to him, enveloping him in expensive perfume that made him cough. "I'll talk to you again later, in a more . . . personal environment, okay?"

He cleared his throat. He wished to goodness that she'd just leave. "KK," he said, using a gamer's abbreviation for "okay."

She glared at him. "Those abbreviations are silly. You play those stupid video games, too, like your brother, don't you?" she demanded. "Well, that's another thing you'll have to work on. No woman is going to tolerate a man who games in every free minute!"

"Unless she's a gamer, too," Joceline said, smiling sweetly. "So many of us women are, these days."

Jon gaped at her.

Charlene glared at her. "It figures," she said curtly.

Joceline kept smiling. She stared pointedly at the other woman's haircut. "My goodness, did your head get caught in a blender or something?"

Jon coughed enthusiastically, trying to conceal laughter.

"I'll have you know I paid a hundred dollars for this styling cut!" Charlene raged.

Joceline held out a hand. "Please lower your voice, ma'am," she urged. "This is a federal office. No verbal outbursts are allowed."

Charlene glanced from one of them to the other with exasperation. "I will never come here again! I'll see you at Cammy's house, when you have time for civilized conversation," she said haughtily.

Jon didn't answer her. Joceline pointedly held the door open and smiled vacantly.

"Have a nice day," she told the departing woman.

Charlene was muttering to herself as she reached the outer office.

Jon let out the laugh he'd been concealing. "That was rude," he told Joceline.

She gave him a blank stare. "Was it, really?" She glanced toward the door. "Should I call her back and apologize?" she asked innocently.

"You do, and you're really fired," he threatened.

She shrugged. "Jobs aren't that hard to get for a woman who knows how to type and give free video game advice," she said. She smiled.

He waved a hand. "Go work on that brief. And what meeting do I have with an informer tonight?" he added with a frown.

"I could arrange one, if you like."

He let out a rough laugh and went back around to sit at his desk. "Cammy's driving me nuts with these prospective brides," he muttered. "I don't want to get married!" he added firmly and glared at Joceline, in the doorway.

She held out both hands. "Don't look at me! I don't want to get married, either. So if you were thinking of asking me," she added outrageously, and with a haughty look, "don't bother. My son would be devastated if we had to try to fit a third person into our Super Mario battles," she added, naming one of the more popular games.

"No worries, there, I like military-themed games."

"And that MMORPG you play with your brother," she told him, referring to federal agent McKuen Kilraven.

"Massively multiplayer online role playing game," he translated and smiled. "I never would have suspected you of being a closet gamer."

She sighed. "Me, either," she replied. "But Markie loves them."

Her son. She had never married, but she'd been going out with a soldier who shipped out to the Middle East and never came back. It had surprised Jon that she'd had a child out of wedlock, when she was such a conservative, religious person. She never spoke of the child's father, and rarely of the child. She kept her personal life as private as Jon kept his own.

Joceline was aware of his curiosity about her. He was dishy, she thought, staring at him unconsciously, with that long, thick black hair in a ponytail down his back and that tall, lean, elegant physique. Women found him attractive, but he was standoffish. Gossip was that he'd never had a woman in his life. Both he and his brother were arch conservatives in just about everything, and neither of them had ever been known for licentious living.

Joceline put that thought out of her mind. She knew things about him that others didn't. In the five years she'd been with the office, watching him work in the field office's Violent Crimes Squad, she often held her breath when he went to work on the kidnapping cases that were his specialty. He had a special interest in human trafficking, particularly of children. He was a bulldog when he was working a case. It was one of many things Joceline admired about him.

Joceline wondered what Jon thought of her morals, knowing that she had a son and no husband. Markie had been a surprise; a shock, really. He was the one beautiful thing in her world, but news of his existence had not been good news at the time. She had told everyone that his father had been a good friend, home on leave from the military, and on the outs with a longtime girlfriend who'd dumped him. Joceline had commiserated with him. They frequently went out together in a platonic way, but that night they'd both had too much to drink. That was her story. But it wasn't quite true.

Joceline had been unsettled and uncertain about going through with the pregnancy at all. There were so many reasons why she should have ended it. But her love for the child's father, who would never know about him, made it impossible to go to a clinic. Such a dangerous, explosive secret she kept . . .

"I said," Jon repeated impatiently, "do you have the case files downloaded into my notebook computer for the court appearance?"

She blinked. "Sorry. What court appearance?"

He scowled. "The one you said I was going to be late for, the Rodriguez child abduction case. I thought it was next week."

"It is next week," she told him, with pursed lips.

He shook his head. "Just as well," he replied. "Another five minutes of discussion

16

on new hairstyles and I think I'd have gone to the window and jumped out."

She gave him a bland look. "We're on the first floor," she reminded him.

"I meant, I'd have jumped out and hit the ground running," he amended.

"Isn't that what Detective Sergeant Rick Marquez did, when a thief stole his laptop?" she recalled, chuckling. "And he got a citation for indecent exposure because he didn't put on any clothes when he went after the man?" She shook her head. "I understand the police department is still riding him high about it."

He chuckled, too. "Marquez is a conundrum. He'll make lieutenant one day, mark my words."

"I believe it."

The phone rang. She smiled, went out and closed the door.

The next morning, Joceline was almost half an hour late for work. When she came in, there were dark circles under her eyes and stress lines in her young face. She was only twenty-six, but she looked much older. She put her purse in her drawer and looked up as Jon appeared, impatiently, in his doorway.

"Sorry, sir," she said in a subdued tone. "I overslept."

His black eyes narrowed. "I haven't said much about it, but this is happening pretty often lately."

She flushed. "I realize that. I'm very sorry."

She was conscientious. She wouldn't do menial tasks, like bringing coffee, but she was the most competent paralegal he'd ever known. She did her job, she never goofed off and she did whatever the work required, even staying late without pay if it came down to it. It wasn't like her to party, so if she overslept, it had to be for another reason.

He came to stand in front of the desk. "What's wrong, Joceline?" he asked in a tone so gentle that tears stung her eyes.

She bit her lip to contain them. "Personal problems, sir," she said huskily. She held up a hand when he started to speak. "I can't . . . discuss them. I'm sorry. I'll try very hard to be on time from now on."

He wondered if her problem was a new man in her life. He didn't like that thought. Then he was surprised that he was thinking it. Joceline was his assistant. Her private life was none of his business. Except that they'd been together for several years and he was concerned about her.

"If you need help," he began.

She smiled stiffly. "Thank you, sir, but I manage very well."

"What do I have on the agenda for today?" he asked, and cleared the way for business.

He was getting ready to leave for lunch with his brother, McKuen Kilraven, when Joceline came to the doorway. She wasn't smiling.

"What's up?" he asked.

She hesitated. "They cut Harold Monroe loose this morning."

He rolled his eyes. "Is my life insurance policy current?" he drawled.

She shook her head. "It isn't funny. I mean, Monroe manages to fumble everything he does, but he did attack a policeman with a Bowie knife when you had him arrested."

It was ironic that another man who'd made terrible threats to Jon earlier in the year had died of a heart attack in prison the day before he was due to be released. Joceline had thought her boss was safe, and had breathed a sigh of relief. But it didn't last. A few days later, Monroe was arrested for human trafficking and charged and swore vengeance against the people who had landed him in jail, including Jon.

"Monroe came at the policeman with a Bowie knife, tripped on the carpet, went head-over-heels and stuck the knife in his own leg," he reminded her with twinkling black eyes. "Then he tried to have the policeman prosecuted for assault."

"I understand some of the people in our legal system are still chuckling over that one," she agreed. "But even people who fumble sometimes manage to follow through on threats."

He waved a hand dismissively. "If he ever kills me, you can stand over my grave and say you told me so. I'm sure I'll hear you from wherever I am."

She didn't like that thought. She averted her eyes. "Anyway, the district attorney's office felt you should be aware of Monroe's parole status."

"I'm very grateful. You can pass that along to Mary Crawford at your leisure."

She grinned. Mary was one of their ablest assistant D.A.s and would probably win the big office one day.

Jon was reading her expressions. "Even if she gets to be D.A., you aren't going to work for her," he said firmly. "I'm too old to start breaking in new employees. The one we've got part-time is twisting my nerves raw."

"Phyllis Hicks is a nice girl," Joceline protested. "Just because she messed up one deposition . . ."

"Messed it up!" he exclaimed. "The woman can't even spell!"

"The spellchecker was malfunctioning," she said defensively.

"Joceline, she's in college part-time. They're supposed to teach you basic grammar in school before you even get to college, aren't they?" He threw up his hands. "Every time I go online, I see people using the contraction for 'it is' for the possessive form, using 'there' for 'their,' giving personal pronouns for inanimate objects . . . !"

She held up a hand. "Sir, we can't all be brilliantly literate. And there is the spellchecker function on all modern computers."

He glared at her. "Civilization will fail. You mark my words. If people can't spell, it's just a short jump to not being able to read instructions at all. Havoc will result."

It was his pet peeve. She just shook her head. "Havoc can't result from not reading instructions."

"Wait until some idiot strikes a match next to an oxygen tank and tell me that again."

Her eyes brightened. "There was this guy on the *Miami Vice* TV series — I have it on DVD — who walked into an illegal drug processing operation with a lit cigarette and blew up the whole building . . . !"

"Don't tell me. You still watch the *A-Team*, too." He rolled his eyes.

"They had to knock out B.A., Mr. T's character, every time they flew somewhere because he was terrified of airplanes," she chuckled.

"There are all sorts of programs on television," he began.

"Yes. How wonderful for people who can afford cable or satellite reception." She sighed dreamily. "It's wonderful to have a DVD player, even if it's old."

He was shocked. He'd never inquired about her finances. But now he took a closer look at her. Her clothing seemed serviceable, but quite old. Not that he cared much about women's fashions, but what she was wearing seemed several years out-of-date. Her shoes were nicely polished, but worn and scuffed.

She blushed when she noticed his intent scrutiny. "There's nothing wrong with dressing conservatively," she muttered.

His eyebrows arched. "God forbid they should put you in stocks," he commented.

"We don't live in Massachusetts and we aren't mucking about in the seventeenth century," she pointed out.

"Point taken." He sighed. "Is my brother going to pick me up for lunch?"

She put a finger to her forehead and closed her eyes. "I see a black SUV pulling into the parking lot as we speak." She opened one eye and looked past him out the window.

He threw up his hands and walked out the door.

Joceline grinned to herself. She liked winding him up. She did it often. He was far too somber. He needed to loosen up a little and stop taking life too seriously.

Then she thought about her own situation and sighed. It was just as well that she had a sense of humor, or she'd be dead herself. Her life was no bed of roses. However, it was just as well to smile as to cry. Neither would change anything.

"You're out of sorts again," Kilraven mused, eyeing the brother who resembled him so much. Well, they had the same hair color, but Kilraven kept his hair short, and Jon's eyes were very dark, where Kilraven's were pale gray and glittery. They were half brothers, but that didn't stop them from being close.

"Cammy's getting on my nerves," Jon said tersely. "It was another dizzy debutante yesterday morning. I had half an hour on fashion and hairstyles."

Kilraven glanced at him as he pulled into traffic. "You could use a little fashion sense. No offense." He chuckled.

"I dress quite well, thank you," Jon said, referring to his three-piece watered gray silk suit.

"You're elegant, all right," said Kilraven, dressed in khaki slacks and a white polo shirt. "But your hair's way out of style."

"I'm Lakota," he pointed out. "Nothing wrong with long hair."

"You're Cherokee, too," came the droll reply.

Jon sighed. "I like my roots and my culture."

Kilraven smiled. "So do I."

Jon glanced at him. "You don't show it."

He shrugged. "I'm not defined by my ancestry."

Jon glared. "Neither am I. But I prefer the Native American side of it."

"I wasn't making accusations," the older man said blithely. "You're just bent out of shape because Cammy wants you to get married yesterday and present her with a dozen grandkids."

"Aren't you and Winnie working on that?" Jon asked dryly, referring to Kilraven's new wife, Winnie Sinclair from Jacobsville.

24

Kilraven chuckled. "Yes, we are. I can't wait."

"I'm glad you can finally let go of the past," Jon said with affection. Kilraven's wife and child had been brutally murdered seven years earlier. He'd never dreamed that his older brother would ever get married again. It delighted him that Kilraven had found such a kind and loving partner.

"You ever going to get married?"

Jon grimaced. "Not to any of Cammy's idiot candidates."

He laughed. "This one wasn't from an escort service . . . ?"

"I don't know." He pursed his lips. "I need to have Joceline run a background check on her, just to see."

"Illegal, unless she's applying for a job with the Bureau."

Jon lifted an eyebrow. "Aren't you a stickler for rules, when you're notorious for breaking them?"

"Hey, we all mature. Some of us just do it later than others."

"True."

"Have you bought the new Halo game?"

Jon smiled. "I bought it a long time ago, but it's still sitting on the shelf at home."

"You and World of Warcraft." Kilraven sighed, shaking his head. "My young brother-in-law, Matt, is crazy for it. When he's not in school, he's online, grouping with other people to kill monsters. His latest friend is a sixty-four-year-old grandmother of three. They do dungeons together."

Jon whistled. "Does she know his age?"

"Oh, yes. And he also plays with a group from a nursing home. They all have internet connections, and most of them play WoW. It's their sole entertainment now, since they're physically handicapped and can't socialize with the world at large." He smiled. "You know, that's not a bad thing. It keeps their hand and eye coordination going, and gives them a window into the whole world."

"I know. I play, too. What's Matt's WoW gamer handle?"

"One of his toons is an eightieth-level Death Knight named Kissofdeaths," Kilraven said.

Jon's eyes bulged. "That's Matt? I've been doing random dungeons with him! He tanks and I heal with my druid."

"I'll have to tell him. He'll roll on the floor laughing."

"Don't you dare," Jon warned. "Now that I know who he is, I'll ride him high."

Kilraven pulled into the parking lot of a local Mexican restaurant and turned off the vehicle. He looked at Jon. "They cut Harold Monroe loose," he said quietly.

"Don't you start. Joceline told me already. She's worried, too. Listen," he said with faint exasperation, "the guy is a total idiot. He can't even walk and chew gum at the same time!"

"He's had his finger in every illegal pie in San Antonio for years. He's been accused of petty theft, running a gambling operation, not to mention houses of prostitution, and now this latest charge, pimping immigrant girls. He sleazed out of the other charges, but you and Joceline tracked down witnesses to have him prosecuted for kidnapping the teen daughter of illegal immigrants for a local brothel," the older man said grimly. "He swore that he'd have the case dropped and he'd get even if he ever got out. He's been in jail for three months waiting trial and he's already spent more time in solitary confinement than any other prisoner they've got."

"Which only proves that he gets caught every time."

"That won't do you much good if he gets caught after he's offed you," Kilraven reminded him.

"I'm street smart," Jon said. "I have built-in radar when it comes to possible

27

ambushes. You should remember that I've never had a speeding ticket."

"At the speeds you travel, I'm still amazed."

Jon grinned. "I always know where they're hiding to catch people."

That was true. It had dumbfounded Kilraven the first time Jon told him to slow down because there was a Department of Public Safety car sitting under a bridge over the next hill. Kilraven had just laughed, but he slowed down. Sure enough, when they topped the hill, there was the car, backed under a bridge out of sight.

"Some ability, and you a cop," Kilraven accused.

Jon shrugged. "It wouldn't do for a senior FBI agent to be caught for speeding in his own jurisdiction," he said.

"You shouldn't be speeding in the first place," Kilraven reminded him.

"Everybody speeds. I just don't get caught."

"There will come a day," his brother predicted.

"When it does, I'll pay the fine," Jon replied. "Are we going to eat or talk?"

Kilraven popped his seat belt and opened the door. "Okay, hide your head in the sand about Monroe. But please keep your doors locked at night and be aware of your surroundings when you're working late."

"You're worse than Cammy."

"I am not," Kilraven said huffily. "I haven't sent one single unattached woman to your office for nefarious purposes."

"I guess you haven't."

They walked toward the restaurant. "I don't suppose you've ever noticed what's right under your nose."

"What do you mean?"

"Joceline," Kilraven replied easily. "She's a fine young woman. Needs a helping hand with her fashion sense, but she's intelligent and quick-thinking."

"You just like her because she knows sixteenth-century Scottish history," Jon accused, because the subject was his brother's passion.

"She knows European history, as well. And seventeenth-century American history."

"Yes, she was spouting it to Cammy's candidate yesterday. She tied her up in knots. The woman was going on and on about fashion and Joceline cut her off at the ankles with historical references to dress codes."

"Told you she was smart."

"She is smart." He looked at Kilraven.

"But I don't want to get married. Not for years yet. I'm just thirty!"

"Almost thirty-one, little brother," Kilraven said affectionately. "And you really don't know what you're missing."

"If I don't know, I can't miss it. Now let's get something to eat," he said quickly, cutting the other man off.

Kilraven chuckled as he followed him into the restaurant. Jon had actually taken Joceline on a date once, some years back. It had been a strange aftermath, including a hospital visit and some threats of legal charges. Jon never spoke of it. He kept secrets. But so did his brother. No doubt he didn't like remembering that his drink had been spiked right under his nose.

2

"But she's such a sweet girl," Cammy argued over the phone. "She's pretty and she knows all the right people!"

"She spent thirty minutes giving me news bulletins on the latest fashions and hair-styles," Jon muttered.

There was an exasperated sigh. "At least she's better dressed than that acid-tongued secretary of yours!"

"Administrative assistant," Jon corrected. "And Joceline at least manages within her budget. She doesn't have to borrow to buy clothes."

"It does show," came the sarcastic reply.

Jon frowned. "Cammy, don't you remember being poor?" he asked quietly.

"I do remember, and I'm your mother, so stop calling me by my first name."

"Sorry, force of habit. Mac does it all the time."

"Call him McKuen, if you please. I hate

that nickname."

"So does he."

"Your secretary has a child out of wedlock," Cammy continued, unabated. "I hate having you associated with someone like that."

He felt himself bristling. "We live in the twenty-first century," he objected.

"Yes, and morality is all that separates us from savagery," she shot back. "We have rules of conduct to keep civilization from floundering. Just look around you at the outrageous things people are doing! Women don't raise children anymore, they run corporations! Do you wonder why the crime rates among juveniles are so high? Who's teaching them values? Who's . . . ?"

He cleared his throat. "Cammy, I'm due in court."

She stopped short, still seething. "You should get another secretary."

"I'm so glad you called. Have a nice day. I'll phone you on the weekend."

"Come to the ranch for the weekend," she suggested.

Where her candidate would be waiting with glee.

"Afraid I can't, there's a stakeout."

"You're a senior agent, surely you can delegate!"

"Not on this one. Now I have to go. Really."

"I don't like it that you work on that violent crimes squad. You could work white collar crime! Jon . . ."

"Bye, Cammy!"

"Don't call me . . . !"

He put down the receiver and let out a puff of air. That was when he noticed Joceline, outside the door he'd forgotten to close. She was very pale and she didn't speak. She walked in, forced a smile and laid a document on his desk. While he was trying to find something to say, and worrying about how much of that conversation she'd overheard, she walked out and closed the door.

Joceline sat down at her desk heavily and tried to block out the sound of Jon's mother's voice, which had been audible even several feet away from the telephone. Most agents used cell phones, and eavesdropping wasn't really possible, but Jon used a landline in the office. And Cammy Blackhawk's voice carried. Joceline felt sick to her stomach as she registered the other woman's overt hostility toward her.

She knew that people talked about her. Gossip was unavoidable in her situation, even in modern times, in a city. Cammy

Blackhawk was a throwback to another generation, one just slightly less tolerant and open-minded than younger people today. It didn't help that Joceline was hopelessly in love with her attractive boss, or that she had uncomfortable dreams about him.

He enjoyed being single. He rarely dated, and even when he did, it was usually a professional woman, an attorney or a district court judge. Once it had been an attractive public defender. But it was usually only one date. Like the one he'd had with Joceline. She didn't dare think too much about that.

She was curious about why he didn't date. She couldn't ask him, of course. It was far too personal a question. But she'd overheard him talking to his brother once about how aggressive women could be. Knowing that his supposedly chaste reputation was like a red flag to a permissive female, she imagined that he'd been faced with imminent seduction more than once and didn't like it. As his mother was moral, so was he. They were both conservative to the back teeth, in fact.

Joceline looked at the photo of Markie that she kept in her wallet. He was a mix of his mother and father. He had his father's elegant straight nose and his black hair. His father was good-looking, and smart. She hoped that Markie would follow his father in that respect.

She sighed over the photograph. Her fascination with her pregnancy had grown by the day while she carried Markie. He was a beautiful child, blue-eyed and slender, with a mischievous expression that was characteristic of him. He loved to play hide-and-seek. He enjoyed video games, especially Super Mario Brothers. He was constantly begging for a puppy or a kitten, but she'd explained gently that it was impossible. He was in day care while she worked, although now he was in preschool part of the day, and day care the rest, and they had no yard for a dog to play in. They had no room, either. It was a one-bedroom apartment, and Markie slept in a small bed near hers. It was wiser that way at night, due to medical problems that she'd never shared with her boss. She worried about her child constantly. There were good medications for his condition, but the ones she used didn't seem to work, especially in the spring and fall of the year. The leaves were just starting to fall in San Antonio as the weather turned cooler, and Markie was having more trouble than usual. It was no wonder that she had dark circles under her eyes and was late to work. Especially after a night like last night . . .

". . . I said, did Riley Blake call?" Jon repeated.

Joceline jumped and dropped the small plastic photo insert she'd been holding.

Frowning, Jon picked it up. He stared at the child in the photograph with curiosity. "He looks like you," he said finally as he handed the insert back to her.

She put it away quickly. "Yes," she stammered. "Sorry, sir."

He shoved his hands in his pockets and stared at her with open curiosity. "We have those bring-your-child-to-work days here, but you never bring your son with you."

"It would be inconvenient," she said. "Markie is a bit of a pirate when he's in company. He'd be making hats out of files and standing on the desk," she added with a laugh.

His eyebrows arched. Cammy had said that Jon had been singularly mischievous as a young boy.

Joceline glanced at him. "They think he may have attention deficit disorder," she said. "They wanted to put him on drugs. . . ."

"What? At his age?" he exclaimed.

She shifted. "He's in preschool," she said. "He unsettles the other children because he's hyperactive."

"Are you going to let them medicate him?" he asked, with real interest.

She looked up, her blue eyes troubled. "I don't know," she said hesitantly. "It's a hard issue to deal with. I thought I'd discuss it with our family doctor and see what he thinks, first."

"Wise." He drew in a long breath. "That's a decision I'd have a hard time with, too."

She managed a smile. "Times have changed."

"Yes."

She searched his black eyes and her body tingled. She looked away quickly. This would never do. She fumbled her purse back under her desk. "I was going to print out that brief for you," she said, opening a file on the computer. "And you're having lunch with the deputy sheriff in that potential federal kidnapping case."

"Yes, we thought we'd discuss the case informally before lawyers become involved."

She gave him a droll look. "I thought you were a lawyer."

"I'm a federal agent."

"With a double major in law and Arabic studies and language."

He shrugged. His dark brows drew together. "How did you manage college?"

She blinked. "Excuse me?"

"You work endless hours and you have a small child," he said. He didn't add that he knew her finances must have been a problem, as well.

She laughed. "I went on the internet. Distance education. I even got a degree that way."

"Amazing."

"It really is," she agreed. "I wanted to know more about a lot of subjects." Her favorite was sixteenth-century Scotland. One of her other interests was Lakota history, but she wasn't telling him that. It might sound awkward, since that was his ancestry.

"Sixteenth-century Scottish history," he mused. He frowned. "You didn't have a case on my brother, did you? That's his passion."

She gave him a glowering look. "Your brother is terrible," she said flatly. "Winnie Sinclair must have the patience and tolerance of a saint to live with him."

He glared at her. "My brother is not terrible."

"Not to you, certainly," she agreed. "But then, you'll never have to marry him."

He chuckled.

"My mother was a MacLeod," she added. "Her people were highland Scots, some of whom fought for Mary Queen of Scots when she tried to regain the throne of Scotland after being deposed by her half brother, James Stuart, Earl of Moray."

"A loyalist."

She nodded. "But my father's family were Stewarts with the Anglicized, not the French, spelling, and they sided with Moray. So you might say they united warring clans."

"Did your parents fight?"

She nodded. "They married because I was on the way, and then divorced when I was about six." Her eyes became distant. "My father was career military. He remarried and moved to the West Coast. He died performing maneuvers in a jet with a flying group."

"Your mother?"

"She remarried, too. She has a daughter . . . a little younger than me. We . . . don't speak."

He frowned. "Why?" he asked without thinking.

"I had a child out of wedlock," she said. "When she found out, she disowned me. She's very religious."

He made a rough sound. "I thought the purpose of religion was to teach forgiveness and tolerance. Besides all that, didn't you just say she was pregnant with you when your father and she got married?"

"Well, it doesn't work out that way sometimes with religion, and the important point to her was that she was married when I was born. We were never really close," she added. "I loved my father very much." She cleared her throat and flushed. "Sorry, sir, I didn't mean to speak of such personal issues on the job."

"I was encouraging you to," he replied quietly. He studied her with open curiosity. "You love your son very much."

She nodded. "I'm glad I decided not to end the pregnancy . . ." She almost bit her tongue off. She grabbed the phone and pushed in numbers. "I forgot to make your lunch reservations!"

Which she never did, considering it a menial chore. But he didn't mention that. He'd upset her by asking personal questions. It hadn't been intentional. He wondered about her private life, about the child.

While she was talking, he went back into his office. He'd meant to apologize to her for Cammy's rudeness, which he was certain that she'd overheard. Then he'd been distracted by the photo of her child. She had thought of ending her pregnancy. Why? She seemed very maternal and conscientious to him, but perhaps she'd never wanted to be pregnant. Accidents did happen. It was just that his clearheaded administrative assistant didn't seem the sort to have amorous accidents, of any type. In the past four years, he didn't recall seeing her date anyone at all.

He sat down behind his desk and recalled her pregnancy. The Bureau didn't discriminate, although her condition hadn't gone down well with some people. But she'd been very quiet, very discreet, during the time she carried the child.

She'd almost died having the child, he recalled. It had disturbed him when he got his first look at her afterward. She'd been pale, listless, devastated by the ordeal.

He'd put that reaction down to pain and drugs following the caesarian section, but now he wondered even more about her history, about the shadowy father of her child.

The phone rang. He picked it up.

"It's Sergeant Marquez," Joceline said formally and put him through.

"Marquez," Jon said. "What are you up to?"

"If you're going to mention my run-in with the computer thief, don't you dare," came the dry reply. "I've already been the subject of extreme censure from everybody up to and including the mayor."

"Really? Perhaps they had a glimpse of you running nude down the street and were impressed."

"Get a life, Blackhawk, you're just jealous of the attention I got," Marquez scoffed. "I'll bet if you ran nude down a street, nobody would even notice you!"

Jon laughed uproariously. "We'll never know."

"Anyway, what I called to tell you is that Harold Monroe beat the human trafficking charges with a hotshot public defender and got cut loose after the parents suddenly refused to testify," he said. "I know the D.A.'s office probably notified you, but sometimes they're slow. I wanted to make sure you knew."

"You're not the first person to tell me. The guy's a total loon and incompetent at that. He can't walk and chew gum at the same time."

"Even people who fumble can perform amazing feats," Marquez said. "You watch your back."

"I'll paint a target on it, so Monroe won't have so much trouble finding me." Jon chuckled. "Thanks for the concern, though. I appreciate it."

"No problem. You still following soccer?"

"Not so much. My video game is taking over my life."

"I heard." There was a pause. "You helped

a tenth-level warrior get a bag to carry his loot in, over in the Barrens."

Jon's eyes popped. "Yes."

"It was one of my alts," Marquez chuckled. "See? You never know who you're playing with."

"Which reminds me, did you know that my brother's brother-in-law plays, too? He's got an 80 death knight." He gave the name.

"Good grief, he fought the Horde with me in Darkshore a few months ago on the pier, before it was destroyed when the expansion came out!"

"He's formidable."

"I'll say, he saved my butt. You just never know, do you?"

"That's what makes it so exciting." Jon hesitated. "You ever going to get married?"

"Look who's talking! Wasn't your last date that public defender who only went out with you to try to get information to save her client?"

Jon's face hardened. "Yes."

"She should have known better. I thought she was a little young for you."

"Twenty-two, to my thirty, almost thirty-one. That's not so much."

"It's a generation." Marquez chuckled. "But she had an agenda."

"It almost got her disbarred."

"At least you didn't have her taken out of your office in handcuffs."

"That woman was a call girl," Jon snapped. "I can't even tell you what she did, and in my own damned office! It was all my mother's fault."

"Cursing in a federal office is not correct behavior and could get you censured by the SAC, sir," Joceline's blithe tone came over the phone.

"Stop eavesdropping!" Jon railed at her.

"And raising your voice is another infraction of the rules of common courtesy," she reminded him.

"Joceline!" he growled.

"There's a public defender out here who wants to speak to you."

Jon hesitated. Marquez was chuckling softly.

"Oh, not that one," Joceline replied at once, with a laugh in her tone. "This one is male and quite handsome."

Why did that anger him? "I'll see him in a minute. Send him to the canteen and show him where the coffeepot is."

"That would be a menial chore, sir," Joceline replied blithely. "As you know, I don't perform menial chores. It's not in my job description." She hung up.

Jon slammed his hand on the desk. "One

day I'll have you hung on the flagpole!" he growled.

"Temper, temper," Joceline said, sticking her head in the door. "You'll ruin the finish on your desk. I asked Agent Barry to show the visitor to the coffee." She gave him a smug look. "Apparently agents don't mind making coffee. Is that in your job description?"

He picked up a magazine and hefted it, with glittery black eyes.

She closed the door with a snap. "Assault with a deadly weapon . . . !" came through it.

"A gaming magazine isn't a deadly weapon!"

"Gaming magazines are against agency policy . . ."

Curses ensued.

"Sir!" Joceline exclaimed haughtily.

Jon actually groaned. Marquez was laughing outrageously.

"One day I'll pour my lunch over her head," Jon muttered.

"Make sure it's something delicious," Marquez suggested. "I'll let you get back to the wars. Just wanted to make sure you knew about Monroe."

"Thanks. I really mean it."

"Hey, what are friends for?" the other man

asked. "See you."

He hung up.

Jon glared at the closed door before he got up and opened it.

Joceline was sitting at her desk, looking angelic. His indignant expression made her bite her lower lip. It would never do to laugh.

The public defender, a slender young man with his blond hair neatly trimmed, came down the hall carrying a plastic cup with black coffee in it. He made a face.

"Don't you have anybody here who can make a decent cup of coffee?" he complained. "You could take rust off old cars with this stuff."

"I make excellent coffee," Joceline said dryly.

The visitor looked at her. "Why aren't you making it, then?"

"It's not in my job description, sir," she said with a vacant smile. "I don't do menial tasks."

"You're his secretary, and you won't make him coffee?"

"I am not a secretary, I'm an administrative assistant and a paralegal," Joceline corrected. "And Mr. Blackhawk would faint on the floor if I ever did such an odd thing here."

"I wouldn't faint," Jon said indignantly. He paused. "I'd have heart failure."

"Fortunately I know CPR," Joceline said. "You're safe with me, sir."

Jon glared at her.

"Don't make an enemy of her," the public defender suggested. "If you drink coffee like this for long, you may have need of her medical training." He made a face and put the cup down on Joceline's desk.

"Please don't do that," she told him. "I'm not responsible for unsupervised beverages. If it spilled on a computer, the agency would have to ask you to replace it."

"How would it spill on a computer?" he asked.

Joceline's hand moved toward it. "It's sitting in a very bad place," she said, and indicated the laptop computer just inches away. "If my hand slipped . . ."

The public defender removed the coffee with a grimace. "I never," he began.

"Give me that." Jon took the cup of coffee, walked down the hall and dumped it into a potted ficus plant.

"How cruel!" Joceline accused when he returned and tossed the empty cup into the trash can beside her desk. "What did that poor plant ever do to you?"

"Nobody ever waters it," he muttered. "It

won't complain. And don't you dare," he added narrowly.

She cleared her throat. "I don't even know anyone who has connections to plant abuse societies."

"With my luck you'd start one," Jon muttered. "Come in. Harris, isn't it?" he asked the public defender as he opened his office door.

"Bill Harris," the defender said, nodding.

"Have a seat. Now what is it you need to discuss?"

Joceline was late because she had to finish typing up three letters, and then print them out since Jon needed hard copies of them. The printer ran out of ink and it took her forever to find the cartridges. Then it ran out of paper and she had to open another carton. She was looking at her watch and grimacing when she finished. She only had ten minutes to get to the day care facility before it closed. The owner was going to be furious. She'd been warned about this once before.

"What is it?" Jon asked when he noticed her expression.

"I have ten minutes before the day care closes," she began.

"Get out of here," he said easily. "I'll finish up."

She hesitated.

"Go on!"

She grabbed her purse. "Thank you, sir."

"No problem."

She made it, but with only two minutes to spare. The taut expression on the owner's face when she arrived spoke volumes. Joceline was worried even more because there had been complaints about Markie's behavior at the day care.

"If this happens again . . ." the woman began.

"It won't," Joceline promised. "I'll arrange for someone to pick him up, if I'm ever asked to stay late again."

The owner sighed. "You work for a federal office. I suppose you can't keep regular hours."

"It's difficult," Joceline agreed. "I need the job too much to refuse overtime."

"My husband was a federal agent, many years ago," the woman said surprisingly. "He was always on call."

"I suppose it was rough for you, too."

The woman looked surprised.

"I know the wives of a couple of our agents, including our Special Agent in Charge. They bite their fingernails when

49

we're on dangerous cases."

The woman smiled. "I had two children and I couldn't afford to put them in day care, so I stayed at home until they started school. Then I couldn't find day care I could afford afterward, so I started my own business."

Joceline smiled. "A wise solution."

The woman nodded. She drew in a breath. "If you have to be late like this again, just call me. I have a girl who left to raise her own children. She'd be happy to keep Markie and she'd pick him up for you. Would you like her phone number?"

"Yes," Joceline said at once, and wondered how she'd afford it.

She wrote the number down and gave it to Joceline. She smiled. "It won't cost you an arm and a leg."

"Your fees are unbelievably reasonable," she pointed out.

The older woman chuckled. "Because I had to afford day care myself," she replied. "I thought there should be a way to make it affordable to people on strangled budgets."

"I'm very grateful." Joceline grimaced. "My budget has gone past strangled to near homicide."

"You could ask that handsome boss of yours for a raise."

"How do you know he's handsome?" she asked.

"His picture was in the paper after he and another agent caught one of the human traffickers they were looking for. Makes me sick what some people can do to helpless poor people in the name of profit. Imagine, using little kids in brothels . . ." She smiled. "Sorry, I hate people who exploit children. I tend to stand on a soapbox on the subject. I'll get Markie for you."

She brought the little boy out a couple of minutes later.

"Mommy!" Markie laughed, holding out his arms to be taken. "I learned how to draw a bird. Miss Ellie taught me! She said I did it real good!"

"You'll have to show me. Tell Mrs. Norris good-night."

"Good night, Mrs. Norris," he said obediently, and smiled at her before he did a nosedive with his face into his mother's throat and held on tight.

"Thanks," Joceline said.

The older woman shrugged. "Men have no idea how tough it is on women who work," she replied.

"None at all," was the quiet reply.

"I had fun!" Markie said when they went into the small, sparsely furnished apartment and Joceline put the three door locks in place. "I got to show you my pictures!"

He handed her a file folder.

She sat down, worn to the bone, and opened it with no real enthusiasm. What she saw shocked her.

"Markie!" she exclaimed. "You drew this?"

"Yes! I saw that bird outside and I drawed him."

"Drew him," she corrected absently.

"It's a . . ."

". . . a goldfinch," she said for him, noting the bright yellow color of the small male bird and its subdued black markings. In the winter, the coat would turn from yellow to the dull green that characterized females.

"You like birds," he said, leaning on her knees while she looked through the drawings. "You got all sorts of books about them. And binoculars." He rubbed his head against her arm. "Couldn't I look through the binoculars again? I want to see if we got any of these birds at our house."

"We probably don't have goldfinches," she replied, because there was no room in her budget for the special seed that constituted the best finch feed. It was outrageously expensive.

"You could cook some bread for them," he said. "You cook real good."

52

"Thank you, sweetheart," she said, and bent to kiss his thick black hair.

"I like pancakes. Couldn't we have pancakes?"

She looked at his rosy cheeks, his big eyes, his sweet expression. He was her whole life. Amazing how he'd changed it, from the first time she looked at him. "Yes," she said, indulging him as she always did, probably too often. "Bacon and pancakes and syrup. But only because I'm so tired," she added.

He smiled. "Thanks, Mom!"

"You're welcome."

The other drawings were also of birds. Just sketches, but they showed great promise of a talent that could be developed. She needed to find him an art teacher if he continued to have interest in the subject.

But that would cost money and she had nothing left over at the end of the week. She sighed. At least she had Markie, she reminded herself. The rest was just superfluous.

3

The public defender, Harris, was trying to get his client a job. It wasn't really his concern, but the young man in question was just twenty years old and already had a wife and a small child. He'd been prosecuted on a bank robbery charge, which put him in the crosshairs of the FBI. He was arrested, charged, jailed, prosecuted and convicted. Now he was out on parole for good behavior after some spectacular legal footwork by this attorney. It had been one of Jon's cases.

"He got drunk one night with some friends, who knocked over a branch bank when it opened early one morning," Harris said. He toyed with his napkin in the restaurant where he'd invited Jon Blackhawk for dinner. "He drew five to ten, even though he was asleep in the backseat the whole time."

"Rough," Jon said.

"It's my first real case," the younger man

said. "I want to do a good job." He glowered. "Substance abuse is responsible for so many problems in our society."

"They did try to ban alcohol once," Jon remarked.

Harris chuckled. "Yes, with interesting results. The only people who got rich during Prohibition were the gangsters."

"That's usually what happens when you declare something illegal. Is it a first offense for your client?"

Harris nodded. "He taught Sunday School, actually."

"I know a minister who was involved in a murder," Jon said, tongue-in-cheek.

Harris laughed. "I know what you mean. But this kid was straight from the time he was old enough to walk. I talked to every relative he had and several friends, not to mention educators who taught him, vouched for him."

"That's a lot of legwork."

"Yes, it is, and I did it on my own time. I believe in this kid. I want to help him. If I can get him a job, and make him understand that he has to stay away from his so-called friends, who are also out on parole, he might have a chance. He's got a three-year-old kid," he added heavily. "And a sweet young wife who adores him."

"Sad case." Jon was noncommittal. He'd heard this story so many times it was grating. It usually ended badly. But he wasn't going to tell this naive but passionate new attorney that. Ideals should be worth something.

"The boy lives in Jacobsville. I thought, since your brother worked in Jacobsville with Cash Grier he might be willing to talk to the local parole officer and put in a good word for him, mention the bad crowd that he got in with and see if there's some way he can be kept away from it," the public defender said hopefully. "A good talking-to at the outset of his parole might do some good."

Jon laughed. "It might at that. Okay. I'll ask him."

Harris brightened like a lightbulb turning on. "Thanks! I owe you one."

"None of us in law enforcement want to see a man fail for one mistake. However," he added solemnly, "if he steps out of line again, you'll be talking to a brick wall if you ask for help."

"I know that."

Jon smiled. He'd talk to Mac. But he knew how this was going to go down, all the same.

"The guy's a born loser," Mac said predictably when Jon phoned him. "If he's stupid enough to be led into crime, he'll stay there. He's a follower with no sense of judgment about other people."

"I don't doubt it. But I promised Harris I'd ask you to intervene. If the kid can be kept away from his old associates, it might help. You can say no. It's not my problem."

Mac sighed. "I suppose I could talk to Grier," he said grudgingly. "But if Harris's client gets into any more trouble, ever, I'll be his worst nightmare."

"I'll be his second worst. Thanks."

"Why are you making your own phone calls?" Kilraven asked suddenly. "Doesn't your AA do that for you?"

"She didn't come in this morning," Jon said, and the worry he felt was reflected in his tone. "Didn't call, either. That's not like her."

"Did you phone her apartment?"

"Yes. No answer."

"Curious. Does she have enemies?"

Jon laughed in spite of himself. "I'm not likely to find her in a sack in the river, if that's what you mean."

"Sorry. I guess I've been in law enforcement too long."

"Join the club. You and Winnie coming to dinner Friday night?"

"Yes, if Cammy isn't going to be there."

"Winnie likes Cammy!"

"I know, but we've both had the tirade from Cammy about her new candidate for your affections. She'll be on a roll and we don't want to spoil a perfect dinner with a lot of argument. If you get what I mean."

Jon chuckled. "I haven't invited her, if that's a help."

"Then you can expect us. Winnie will bring homemade rolls. I didn't ask. She offered."

"I'm amazed she can still manage to bend over the oven with her belly sticking out that far," Jon remarked. "Cammy's sure it's going to be a boy because she's big in front like that."

"Childbirth is a mystery to most people. Not to Cammy. We'll be over about six."

"See you then."

Jon hung up. He hadn't let it show in his tone, but he was worried about Joceline. It was the first time she'd ever missed work without calling first. Something big must be up. He immediately thought of her son.

He picked up the phone and started calling hospitals.

Joceline was pacing the waiting room floor. She'd brought her knitting bag with her, but even that chore hadn't diverted her.

This had been a bad attack, the worst one yet. She'd tried to go into the cubicle with Markie, but the attending physician and a nurse had shooed her out in the kindest way possible. They needed to run tests, they explained.

It was hard to leave a child who sounded as if he were smothering to death. Joceline was beside herself. Markie was her whole life. What if he died this time? What if they couldn't save him . . . ?

"Joceline?"

She jumped and gasped at the sound of her boss's voice behind her. She jerked around, astonished.

"It's not like you," he explained, "not to call, if you can't make it to work. I figured it had to be something catastrophic."

She bit her lower lip. "It's Markie," she said on a long breath. "A bad attack. The worst one he's had yet." She folded her arms over her small breasts. "They're running tests."

At least she had medical insurance, good insurance, from her job. But it wouldn't cover all of the expense, and she didn't know how she'd add another monthly payment to the bills she already had.

"What sort of attack?" Jon repeated. Her mind was busy. She hadn't even heard him.

"He has asthma," she said heavily. "In the spring and fall, colds go down into his chest. He has chest infections, sometimes pneumonia. There are new drugs, good ones, for his condition, and we use them. He has allergy shots every week, too. But his lungs are just weak. He's never had an attack come on so quickly, or be this bad. I didn't think I'd even get him here in time . . ." She bit her lip and turned away.

"Has he seen a specialist?"

"Yes. Lung specialists, allergists, the works." She sighed. "I don't even smoke," she said plaintively.

He wondered how she managed to pay specialists. It would be rough for anyone, but especially for a single mother on a limited budget. He didn't have to be told that a child with uncontrolled asthma was an expensive little person to treat. He'd had his own share of respiratory problems as a child, Cammy had once told him. He still had allergies, too.

Joceline looked worriedly at the door to the emergency room from which a white-coated physician with a stethoscope around his neck had just emerged.

"That's Dr. Wagner," she explained as she moved toward him. "He's our family doctor."

The tall, thin physician smiled as she approached. "It's all right, Joceline, he's doing very well. We'll have the test results for you very soon. You have to stop worrying so much," he added gently. "Odds are very good that he'll outgrow the asthma, and that the allergies will respond to the shots and diminish. It just needs time."

She let out a breath. "I try so hard to make him wear his jacket when it's cool and a raincoat when it's raining," she muttered. "He whips them off the minute he gets out of my sight. Then he catches cold. There was a cold rain yesterday morning, and he went outside during play period without a coat and didn't tell me until he woke up smothering this morning."

Dr. Wagner chuckled. "Don't blame yourself. He's very sorry that he did it, more because of how upset you were than how dangerous it was to him," he added. "He has a big heart for such a small child."

"He gets picked on a lot at school because he can't run like the other kids without getting out of breath," Joceline said heavily. "And because he has to take shots for the allergies. Why are kids so mean to each other?"

"Why are there bullies?" Dr. Wagner replied. "I don't know. I wish it was an issue that could be resolved. Now with cyber-bullying so prevalent, a victimized child can see no peace even in his own home."

"There should be more lawsuits," Joceline muttered.

"I agree," Jon said quietly.

Dr. Wagner looked at Jon curiously.

"This is my boss," Joceline said quickly, so the doctor wouldn't get the wrong idea. "Senior Agent Jon Blackhawk."

Dr. Wagner shook hands. "I wanted to join the FBI myself when I was younger," the doctor said surprisingly, "but my father wanted me to study medicine." He laughed. "In the long run, I suppose he was right. We have four generations of physicians and surgeons in my family. I'd hate to be the one to break the tradition."

"It's lucky for us that you didn't," Joceline said. "Thank you for taking such good care of Markie."

He smiled. "I told you that one day you'd be glad you made the decision you made," he said enigmatically.

"I am, now, more than ever, despite the problems," she added with a weary smile.

"Why don't you go and get something to eat?" the doctor asked. "By the time you get back, Markie will be ready to go home."

"They won't have to keep him?" she worried.

"Oh, I don't think so," he replied. "We just want to make sure he's stabilized and get him started on the new antibiotic. There are new inhalers out also, Joceline, you should talk to his allergist about them. One is for pediatric patients and has shown good results."

She sighed heavily. The allergist had suggested one of the newer inhalers, which was over a hundred dollars a month. On her budget, even with good insurance, that was a fortune. But perhaps she could write to the drug company and request a reduced price. That had worked for her in the past. "Thank God he's going to be all right."

"Nice to meet you, Agent Blackhawk," Dr. Wagner added, smiling as he walked away.

"Nice guy," Jon remarked.

"Yes, we're very lucky to have him. He's taken great care of Markie."

Jon was studying her with narrowed eyes. The doctor's statement about the decision she'd made was puzzling.

She was tired and raw from lack of sleep or she might have reconsidered her words. "His father and I were very good friends. We had too much to drink and . . . there was Markie."

He stared at her. He didn't speak.

She averted her eyes. "I underestimated how —" she started to say "drugged" and immediately caught herself "— drunk he was and he didn't realize that I was naive about men. We were both stupid." She hesitated. "I wasn't sure how I'd feel about a child who wasn't planned." She smiled. "But now he's my whole world." Her voice broke off.

"Your path hasn't been an easy one," Jon said quietly.

"Nobody's path is easy. We just do what we have to do, and go on living. I love my son," she added. "I have to live with the fact that Markie will always be illegitimate." She looked up at him. "It hurts me. I try to live a conservative life. But it's not Markie's fault."

"Of course not."

She picked up her purse from the seat she'd occupied. "I'll get some breakfast and see what they can do for Markie, but I don't know if I can come in today. I'm very sorry. I should have phoned."

"I was concerned," he replied. "Take the day off. If you can't make it in tomorrow, just let me know, it will be all right. The Bureau doesn't punish people for personal emergencies, you know," he offered with a kind smile.

She smiled back. "Thanks," she said.

"Markie's father, is he still alive?"

The question hit her unexpectedly. "I . . . I don't know," she stammered, desperate for a way out of the conversation.

"You said that he was in the military, stationed overseas," he began.

"Yes, I see," she faltered. She averted her eyes. "He was, uh, listed as missing in action."

"A tragedy."

She nodded. "Thanks for coming down here," she said, recovering her poise. "I don't know how you even found us . . ."

"Abuse of power," he quipped. He grinned. "I can pull strings when I want to."

"Unethical, sir," she pointed out.

He shrugged. "My brother is corrupting me."

She laughed. She glanced at the big clock in the waiting room. "You've got a meeting with the sheriff about that Oklahoma kidnapping in ten minutes at the courthouse," she exclaimed, referring to a case in which an agent in another field office had requested some help. FBI offices cooperated on cases from other jurisdictions that overlapped. "You'll never make it."

"I'll make sure I catch all the traffic lights

when they're green." He chuckled.

"Thanks again."

"You're welcome. I'll see you tomorrow."

She nodded. She watched him walk away. It surprised her that he cared enough to hunt her down when she didn't show up for work. And he'd been really concerned. That made her feel warm inside. She fought it. His mother would be the worst enemy on earth to make. Joceline already knew how the woman felt about her. It gave her cold chills. But then she was worrying about things she might not ever have to consider. She had her son, and he was going to get better. That had to be her concern now. Only that.

"I'm really sorry about walking in the rain, Mommy," Markie apologized when they were back home in their small apartment. "I love rain," he added plaintively.

"I know you do, sweetheart, but your lungs don't," she said, trying to explain. "You don't like being sick."

He shook his head. "I don't like making you upset, too." He dived against her side and held on tight. "I love you so much, Mommy!"

"I love you, too, pumpkin," she replied and hugged him back, hard.

"I'll wear my coat next time."

They both knew he was lying. She'd just have to be more careful. It wasn't the rain, the doctor had told her, but the fact that Markie was sensitive to viruses and he'd had one starting when he got wet. It wasn't dangerous for a healthy child, but then, Markie had never been really robust.

The specialist changed his allergy medicines. Joceline talked to the drug company and they agreed voluntarily to give her the inhalers for a fraction of the retail cost. The medication seemed to be working, too. Markie perked up. His valleys and peaks leveled off and he settled into school with resignation. Joceline had a long talk with Markie's teacher and the owner of the day care, and an attorney who was kind enough to help her *pro bono.* For the time being, the bullying was curtailed. But they did mention that Markie was distracting in the classroom and set a date for her to come back, alone, and discuss it with them.

Meanwhile, Markie got better and Joceline got her nerves back together. There was still the question of a diagnosis for Markie's behavioral problems. She didn't know what to do. There was really nobody who could help except their doctor. She'd asked him about Markie and he agreed that it was possible that the child had attention deficit disorder. He was researching the medications and considering a reply for her.

She was doing well until Cammy Blackhawk stormed into the office and glared at Joceline as if she was a hooker.

"I would like to see my son," she said haughtily.

Joceline, practiced at handling gruff and unpleasant individuals, gave her a vacant smile. "Of course, ma'am. Won't you have a seat in our modern and ergonomically designed waiting area?"

Cammy blinked.

Joceline picked up the phone. "Mrs. Blackhawk is here to see you, sir."

Jon came out the door at once, looking oddly protective as he glanced at Joceline and then at Cammy.

"Hi," he said.

Cammy stared at Joceline uncomfortably and then back at her son. "I want you to come to supper tonight," she said firmly. "I'm having a soiree . . ."

"Soiree?" Jon asked, surprised.

"It's a French word, sir," Joceline told him helpfully. "It means a small, informal dinner . . ."

"I know what it means!" he snapped.

She saluted him.

He rolled his eyes. "Cammy, I can't come.

I'm having supper with Mac and Winnie," he said firmly.

"Don't call me Cammy! I'm your mother!" she grumbled.

"And I don't want to try to eat while I'm being regaled with the latest fashion information," he continued irritably.

"Many, many people buy specialized magazines to ferret out that information," Joceline began enthusiastically.

"Do you mind?" Cammy snapped at her. "I am trying to speak to my son!"

Joceline saluted her, too, smiled again and went back to typing on the computer.

"Come in here," Jon muttered, pulling Cammy into his office. He closed the door. "For the last time, I do not want to have supper with your matrimonial candidate!"

"She's a nice girl!"

His narrowed eyes glittered. "I don't want to get married! Winnie's pregnant. Why don't you go and overwhelm her with motherly advice?"

Cammy averted her eyes. "She's getting that from her own mother. I'm superfluous."

"Well, you can advise Mac on being a father," he countered.

"He's always being called away from the phone, and when I try to visit his office, he's always out," she said irritably.

"You're a bulldozer," he told her. "You don't think anyone can live if you're not telling them how to go about it."

"I'm just trying to help," she said, exasperated.

"You should have had more kids," he replied. "It's 'empty nest syndrome.' You're lonely and bored."

"You're all alone," she said miserably. "What will happen to you when I die?"

He was shocked by the question. "Are you planning to?"

She averted her eyes. "Don't be silly. I just want to see you happily married, like Mac is."

"If it had been up to you, Mac would never have married Winnie," he reminded her. "You thought she was after his money."

"So I made an error in judgment," she said, clearly uncomfortable. "But this nice girl is just what you need. She's outgoing and social, always dressed in the latest fashion and she knows many people in high places."

"So do I," he reminded her.

"You need a family. You don't even date anybody. Well," she amended thoughtfully, "there was that lawyer, but wasn't she just trying to get information out of you about a client?"

He didn't like being reminded of that. "I date when I feel like it."

"Yes, but you never feel like it!" she retorted. "You should have children to play with, now while you're still young enough to play with them and do things with them!"

"I'm not married, Cammy," he said patiently.

"I noticed!"

"I lead a hectic life," he continued. "Most women wouldn't be able to put up with the hours I keep."

"Charlene is beautiful and she's very tolerant of your lifestyle," Cammy began.

"She is not," Jon shot back. "She said that I'd have to give up video games."

"You play too many of them," Cammy agreed. "You should have children to take up your spare time."

"Don't you have anything else to do with your life besides trying to run mine for me?" Jon asked finally, exasperated.

"I am not trying to run your life. I want you to be happy."

"Harassing me about marriage isn't doing the job."

"It isn't harassment," she groaned. "Son, you don't even have a social life."

71

"I don't want one. I love my work."

"You always have," Cammy replied heavily. "You and McKuen, burying yourselves in dangerous occupations! The past has taken a heavy toll on both of you."

"And on you," Jon agreed. He kissed her forehead. "I know you miss Dad," he said gently. "So do all of us. But you're going overboard with plans for my future. You have to let life happen. You can't force people to do things they don't want to do."

"You'd like Charlene if you gave her a chance," she argued.

"She's the most opinionated woman I've met recently," he said gruffly.

"You're only upset because she said you'd have to stop playing so many video games," Cammy replied. "And she's right."

"She is not."

"We can agree to differ. You should get out more. You spend too much time in this office with that woman out there," she muttered.

"Joceline is my administrative assistant," Jon replied. "She's also a competent paralegal. Who do you think found the link that solved the murder of Mac's little girl?"

Cammy frowned. "I thought it was McKuen."

He shook his head. "Joceline dug out the

information that broke the case."

Cammy was evidently surprised, and not pleasantly. She shifted her feet. "She's disrespectful."

"I haven't noticed that."

"And she's got a child. She's not married."

"She was going to be. Her fiancé died overseas in the military before he could marry her," he said with faint defensiveness.

"She told you that?"

He nodded.

"How do you know it's the truth?" she asked with a cold smile. "Women tell all sorts of stories."

"Why are you so antagonistic toward her?"

She didn't answer him. "If you won't come to supper, how about to lunch tomorrow?"

"It's a long drive to the ranch," he began.

"I'm staying at the apartment in town," she replied. "You'll come, won't you?"

He wanted a way out, but he was reluctant to refuse. Cammy was his mother. He didn't spend a lot of time with her, and he felt guilty.

"I suppose I could. If it's going to be just the two of us," he added firmly.

"Of course," she replied. She smiled. "Just us two."

"Now, I have work to do," he reminded her, opening the door.

"I'll have something nice for you to eat," she promised. She smiled at him and impulsively hugged him. "That's my good boy. I'll see you tomorrow." She kissed him, shot a cool look at Joceline and breezed out the front door.

"They do make Bengal tiger traps," Joceline said thoughtfully. "Although you would have to dig a deep hole in the office."

He wouldn't smile, he wouldn't smile . . .

She heard a muffled sound from behind his closed door, and she grinned.

That night she took Markie to a local restaurant that featured a video game arcade. It was filled to capacity.

"Let's try this one," she said enthusiastically after they'd had chicken fingers and iced tea. "Here!"

"I like this one," Markie agreed with a grin.

It was piloting fighter planes and shooting at an enemy on a huge movie screen. Markie laughed uninhibitedly, and so did Joceline. She enjoyed the once-a-month outing as much as he did. They had little money for frivolous things like this, but she didn't want Markie to miss out on entertainment that other children had access to. For a four-year-old, he had an amazing dexterity and skill at the game.

She was aware of movement behind her. Suddenly there were three other people in the compartment, parked on either side of her and Markie, putting game cards into the slots.

"Think you're good, do you?" Mac Kilraven chided. "Let's see!"

"Don't let him bait you, Joceline," a very pregnant Winnie Sinclair said and laughed from beside him. "I can outshoot him! So can you!"

"A likely story," Jon Blackhawk scoffed as he manned the console next to Joceline's.

"I thought you were having dinner with them at home," she said to Jon, indicating his brother and sister-in-law.

"We did, but this is our favorite hangout," Jon said. "We like the games."

"If we had a bigger apartment, I'd import some like this." Mac chuckled. "It will be great for the kids."

"Your son seems to like it," Jon commented to Joceline as Markie took down another fighter.

"Look! I hit it!" He laughed.

"Good shot, there," Jon agreed, smiling at the child, who smiled back.

"Get in much practice in real life, do you?" Mac asked the boy with a wink.

"I don't get out much," Markie said in a very adult tone, and with rolled eyes at his mother.

Joceline laughed. "He's not allowed to carry antiaircraft weapons in public," she said, tongue-in-cheek.

"Aw, Mom." Markie sighed. "I never get to have any fun!"

"Tell you what, first enemy fighter jet that dives on you, I'll get you the best missile launcher I can find," Joceline told him.

"Wow," Markie said with pure worship in his eyes. "Thanks, Mom!"

She shrugged. "Nothing's too good for my boy," she said, and winked at him. She fought down her discomfort at having Markie around her boss. She didn't want any problems to crop up, and Jon Blackhawk's mother would be livid if she knew he was even playing video games with his administrative assistant outside work. But she wouldn't know. Hopefully.

4

Joceline and Markie walked toward the exit an hour later. They'd spent the balance on their game cards, although Mac and Jon had subsidized them, in a nice way.

"Thanks," she told Jon at the door. "Markie had so much fun. So did I," she added, but with averted eyes.

"It's all right to admit that you like something I do," he murmured dryly. "You so rarely approve of my actions."

"We wouldn't want you to get a superiority complex, would we, sir?" she asked.

"Why do you call him 'sir'?" Markie asked.

"He's my boss," she replied.

"Oh. Like those guys in the military call their bosses 'sir.' "

"Something like that," Joceline agreed.

"Does he put you in 'time-out' if you do something bad?" Markie persisted.

"I would never do such a thing," Jon assured him. "And your mother has never done anything bad." He hesitated. "Nothing really bad," he amended, giving her a speaking look.

"Menial tasks are not part of my job description, sir," she reminded him. She smiled.

"Making decent coffee isn't menial." He sighed.

"That depends on your definition," she retorted.

"You shoot real good," Markie told the tall man. He was looking pointedly at the bulge under Jon's jacket. "You got a gun."

"That's right," Jon told him. "I work for the FBI."

"I know. Mom talks about you all the time."

"We should go," Joceline said, a little flushed. "Thanks again," she added. "I'll see you Monday, sir."

"Mommy . . ." Markie protested as she rushed him out the door.

Mac had been listening. He glanced at his brother. "Talks about you all the time, huh?"

"I'm sure he meant in a work-related way," Jon said stiffly. "Joceline has worked for the agency for several years."

"So have you."

Jon glared at his older brother. "She works for me. Period."

Mac pursed his lips, but he didn't reply. He just chuckled and went back to the table where Winnie was waiting for him.

Jon was out of humor when he walked into the office Monday morning. Joceline was still putting away her jacket and purse, having only just beaten him to work.

"You're late," he muttered.

She pointed to the clock over her desk. She was absolutely on time. It was eight on the dot.

He shrugged and went into his office to see what he had on his day planner. The phone rang while he was searching it.

His intercom buzzed. "Yes?" he replied.

There was a pause. "It's for you, sir. A Mr. Harold Monroe." She said the name pointedly.

He frowned and picked up the phone. "Blackhawk," he said.

"Hiya," he replied. "Remember me? I'm out now waiting for a new trial. I'll beat that trafficking charge. I got a great lawyer."

"Congratulations," Jon said. "I'll send over balloons."

There was a pause. "Balloons?"

"For the celebration."

"Cele . . . oh. Oh! Ha ha ha."

"Was there something else?"

79

"No, nothing else. I just wanted you to know I was out."

"Thank you."

Another pause. "You made a mistake."

"Did I?"

"Yeah. You want to be careful. My family gets even with people who hurt it. Always. I'll be seeing you, Agent Blackhawk."

He hung up.

Jon stared at the receiver before he replaced it. "It takes all kinds," he muttered.

He was on his way out the door when Joceline called to him.

"Rick Marquez wants you to stop by his office while you're out," she told him. "He says it's important."

"What is it about?" Jon asked, turning.

She put a finger to her forehead and closed her eyes. "I see mountains. Trees. Birds flying." She opened her eyes. "However, not being psychic, I have no idea."

"He didn't say?"

"Apparently not." She smiled vacantly. She cocked her head. "Would you like to know what the new skirt length is out of the Milan fashion shows . . . ? Sir, it's not polite to turn your back on people who are talking to you!" she called after him.

"One day I'll strangle her," Jon muttered to Rick Marquez while they were sitting at

80

the detective's desk, drinking coffee. He'd just related Joceline's latest verbal coup.

Marquez chuckled. "You'd never replace her," he commented. "I've seen paralegals come and go. Joceline is in a class all her own."

"I know." The other man sighed. "I wouldn't have half my cases solved without her. She can dig out information that I can't get. I have no idea how she pulls it off, either."

"She's psychic," Marquez said with big eyes.

"She is not. She's just very good with a telephone, and she can talk people into telling her things that they don't want to."

"She's a paralegal. Why isn't she working for a judge or at least a firm of attorneys?" Marquez asked with a curious frown.

"She started out as legal secretary to a firm of attorneys. But the senior partner retired, several more attorneys joined the firm and she was doing the work of three paralegals with the pay of one," Jon said. "We got her as a result. It was a good thing that Garon Grier didn't have her put on the rack when he started work at the office," he added thoughtfully.

Marquez burst out laughing. "What?"

"He was used to female workers making

coffee for him. Joceline doesn't do menial tasks. Or what she considers menial tasks."

"Our administrative assistants make coffee," Rick said smugly. "Good coffee," he emphasized with a pointed look at Jon.

Jon sighed. "None of us can make drinkable coffee. On a bright note, our potted palm seems to thrive on caffeine."

"Excuse me?"

"Everybody dumps their coffee into it when we aren't looking." He chuckled.

Marquez sighed. "Oh, the adventure of working at a federal office."

"At least we have decent expense accounts," he replied. "We don't have to have a receipt for a cup of ice."

Marquez made a face. "It was a very hot day and our air conditioner wasn't working."

"You're from Mexico originally, and you live in southern Texas. You should be used to the heat," Jon commented.

"Yeah. Go figure." Marquez wasn't comfortable talking about his childhood. In fact, nobody except his adoptive mother, Barbara, in Jacobsville, even knew what his background was. And neither he nor Barbara knew the whole truth, but they were trying to find it. However, he had no plans to share that news with his visitor, even though he liked and respected the FBI agent.

"I didn't mean to offend," Jon said, sensitive to the expression that flashed just briefly across the other man's face. "I know about racial issues. You might have noticed that my ancestry includes feathered headdresses and mounted combat."

Marquez relaxed, and smiled. "So does mine, actually. One of my forebears was Comanche."

"Really? So was one of mine," he replied.

"No kidding? Small world."

"My mother has Cherokee, my father was full-blooded Lakota," Jon said.

Marquez's eyebrows arched. "Cherokees come from back East originally."

"Yes, they were relocated on the 'Trail of Tears.' Cherokees were rounded up in 1838 and removed to Oklahoma in late 1838 and early 1839, in the winter cold and snow without proper clothing, because of gold discoveries." He shook his head. "One of my ancestors said that we could never coexist with a materialist culture, because we shared everything and the conquerors wanted to own everything," he added.

"Interesting thought." He put down his coffee cup and became somber. "Harold Monroe's been hinting about retribution to one of my informants."

"I heard they cut him loose."

"Yes, they did. Like the rest of his family, he has something of a reputation for revenge." He looked pointedly at Jon. "He's been accused of racketeering, gambling, prostitution, you name it, but he's never spent more than a day in jail on any charge. One of the prosecutors in a murder case against his uncle-by-marriage died under mysterious circumstances, along with the only witness, and he was let go. Nothing was ever proven. You had Monroe in jail for several months while his lawyer worked to get the charges dropped."

"He should blame himself for putting little girls in the hands of pimps."

"That's not how he sees things. He said the kid was living in starvation-level poverty. He was just helping her find a better life. Simple."

"Yes. I saw the result of that better life," Jon said without elaborating, but the expression in his eyes was eloquent. "Well, they can drop charges, but I still have witnesses who'll testify. One was the man who sold his daughter to Monroe."

"That's the problem." Marquez grimaced. "The witness says he won't testify and he's withdrawn his statement."

"No problem," Jon said. "I know where we can find three more witnesses in the same family, two of whom are perfectly willing to testify despite any threats from Monroe."

"Give me their names and we'll help you locate them so you can get depositions, since it's a federal charge he was arrested on," Marquez replied. "Why didn't the witnesses come forward before?"

"Because they fell through the cracks," he said. "We had one witness, the father, who gave us a deposition, and the mother, as well as a sister. The federal prosecutor didn't think he needed more than a handful. Now we do." He shook his head. "I hope they don't go the way of the witness who was supposed to testify against Jay Copper at his trial about the death of that teenager in Senator Sanders's case. He accidentally fell off a ten-story building."

Marquez wrote down the names of the witnesses. "We do our best," he said defensively.

"So do we, and it wasn't a criticism. Unless you're really psychic, you can't foresee a murder in your city."

"It would be nice if we could." Marquez sighed. "I just hope Monroe doesn't walk on this one."

"With the federal charges dropped on a technicality," Jon said, grinding his teeth at the so-called technicality, which involved a slipped link in the evidence chain, "and new charges pending, the ball may be in your court if we can't make ours stick. You can still get him for trafficking, though. We'll help."

"He won't walk. I promise." He narrowed his eyes. "But you watch yourself."

"You're giving Monroe too much credit," Jon said. "He's a beer short of a six-pack." He pursed his lips. "Maybe two beers short of a six-pack."

"He may be, but he's dangerous. You got him on a trafficking charge. But he's worked his way out of numerous other charges including one daylight robbery. That one was committed as a juvy —" which meant a juvenile offender "— and he only drew a few days in detention before he turned eighteen."

"Yes, he managed to get first offender status and kept his nose clean until his record was wiped," Jon said. "But he was twenty-five when he was accused the next time, and he got a good attorney, courtesy of his boss, Hank Sanders, the racketeer brother of Senator Will Sanders who's up on murder charges." He smiled. "Hank turned out to be a good guy. He saved my brother's butt in the standoff with Jay Copper, just after Mac and Winnie came back from their honeymoon."

"Some honeymoon, trying to convince Senator Will Sanders's wife, Pat, to tell what she knew about the murder of Kilraven's wife and little girl," Marquez amended.

"Which she did, but Copper ordered the murder of Mac's wife," Jon said somberly. "He said that the perp, the late Dan Jones, wasn't ordered to kill Melly, Mac's little girl, but I never believed him. One of his idiot goons turned state's evidence and verified that Copper told Jones to get both the wife and child. He'll pay for Melly's death, and Monica's. The D.A. has asked for the death penalty."

"Good luck to him," the other man said cynically. "Juries don't like to order it."

Jon nodded. "I had to sit in a death-penalty case once. You think, this guy should die for the crime he committed. But when you put your vote to it, and realize that you're ordering the guy's death, well that's a whole other thing."

"A matter of personal conscience," Marquez agreed. "A very hard decision to make, for any human being." He studied Jon. "But it's you I'm worried about. Monroe may be

87

an idiot, but he has an uncle who's knee-deep in the local mob, Jay Copper, and a brother-in-law who's been in and out of prison for years, Bart Hancock. Hancock walked on accessory charges linked to Jay Copper's arrest, because the tape Winnie got of Copper telling the story of the murders went mysteriously missing. Hancock has been implicated in two murder-for-hire plots and never got much past arraignment. He makes sure there are no witnesses."

"There's something in the back of my mind about Hancock. Wait! Now I remember," Jon said. "Joceline dug up some information on him that was supposedly classified. Don't ask —" he held up a hand "— she has sources. Anyway, Hancock was in spec ops in Iraq during the 2003 invasion."

"That's right. He worked with a private contractor. There was a big stink about civilian casualties, and Hancock was in it up to his neck. His buddy was an officer in the private corporation that ran the coverts, and he cleaned up Hancock's record so he wasn't prosecuted." He sighed heavily. "They say he killed children and enjoyed it."

Jon's jaw set. "What a sweetheart."

"Isn't he, though?"

"Yes."

Jon's mind was busy. The man who died linked to Melly's murder, Dan Jones, was a bit of a mystery. Jon had always wondered if the man was really going to confess that he'd done it. He didn't seem the sort to kill children. But Jay Copper's spec ops nephew, he had been friends with the perp, and the accomplice who'd gone with the perp to commit the murders was never found. What if . . . ?

"You've remembered something, haven't you?" the other man asked, noting the facial expression of his visitor.

Jon nodded. "Yes, that there were two shooters at Mac's house that night. We only identified one. The tape had Jay Copper talking about his nephew, Peppy, who helped Dan Jones kill Monica. He said the child got in the way. Peppy was questioned but he suddenly had a supposedly airtight alibi for that night. Then the tape where Jay Copper told about Peppy's part in the murder went missing from the evidence room . . ."

"I'd forgotten that." Marquez opened a file on his computer and his dark eyes narrowed as he read what was on the screen. "Peppy. His full name is Bartholomew Richard Hancock. And his brother-in-law is Harold Monroe, which makes Monroe Jay Copper's nephew by marriage. I don't have to tell you Copper's reputation for getting back at anyone who works against his family." He glanced at Jon, whose face wore a look of utter astonishment. "You never made the connection, did you?"

It had been four months ago, the end of the trail when all the suspects in Dan Jones's death, and at the same time the Kilraven murders, were fingered. Only Senator Will Sanders and Jay Copper had been arrested and sent to jail pending trial. But the man, Peppy, had slipped out of the noose with the help of a slick attorney and had never been charged even as an accessory, thanks to that missing tape, which, through an unfortunate lapse, had not been copied or transcribed before it was stolen. Jay Copper denied he'd ever implicated Peppy. The fact that Kilraven, and Winnie, were closely involved helped to discount their testimony about it. Pat Sanders had suddenly backtracked on her own testimony, despite the efforts of Hank Sanders, the senator's brother, to coax her to repeat it.

Harold Monroe had been arrested by Jon on the human trafficking charge not a week after Peppy Hancock had slipped out of the accessory murder charge in the Kilraven case. Jon and Joceline had worked tirelessly to find the evidence to connect him with the trafficking, which they'd been investigating prior to his most recent arrest. But no, Jon had never made the connection.

"So Harold Monroe may be an idiot," Marquez agreed, "but Hancock isn't. You want to watch your back. He might target anyone close to you, but especially Joceline, since she helped you get evidence on him. His uncle Jay would know she helped. He has somebody in law enforcement feeding him information. We've never been able to identify who."

Jon sighed. "Why is life so complicated?"

Marquez indicated the office they were sitting in. "This is a police precinct. If you want answers to philosophical questions, you should consult a psychologist."

Jon glared at him. "Thanks a lot."

Marquez grinned. "You're welcome. More coffee?"

Knowing that Peppy, alias Bart Hancock, had possibly been involved in the murder of Mac's daughter, Melly, was like carrying live dynamite to Jon. He didn't know if he should tell his brother at all, at least not until he could do some more checking. If Marquez was right, and he usually was, that meant the murder of Mac's wife and child hadn't been completely solved at all. Mac had thought Jay Copper, having ordered the hit, had been brought to justice and would pay for the child's death. But if Peppy had helped the late Dan Jones with the hit — that was another whole can of worms. And Peppy was married to Harold Monroe's sister. What a mess. A threat Jon had laughed off suddenly became a real possibility, and not just a danger to himself.

He went back to his office and sat down heavily at his desk, staring at the wall opposite. Joceline called him on the intercom and he didn't even hear it. He was sick at his stomach.

She poked her head in the door and frowned when she saw his expression. "Something wrong?"

He nodded. He glanced at her. His black eyes were glittery. "Come in and close the door. Do I have anything urgent pending?"

"No." She closed the door and sat down on the uncomfortable straight chair in front of his desk. No comfortable seats for this boss; he didn't like people overstaying their welcome. She was uncomfortable, too, and not just from the chair. Was he going to fire her? She was a bundle of nerves lately. She had a meeting pending with both Markie's teacher and the owner of the preschool about his behavior. They were going to recommend drugs, she just knew it. She had no money, no option to change his school for a more expensive one. She was in the hot seat and she didn't like it.

"Am I being fired due to budget cuts?" she asked bluntly.

He noted her worried expression. Joceline was a single parent with only the bare necessities and even though she had great prospects, it might take time for her to find a new job.

"Of course not," he said at once.

She relaxed, just a bit. A jerky little smile passed her lips. "Sorry. I worry."

"The talk about budget cuts involves travel, not personnel. At least for now. We all worry, but until they come up with robots who won't mind working our hours, I think we're probably safe as far as employment goes," he said with an attempt at humor. "I need someone to talk to."

"There's your brother," she said. She frowned. "I think we have a psychology consultant in an office somewhere . . . ?"

"Not that kind of talk," he said stiffly. "I don't discuss personal issues except with family."

"Of course you don't, sir." She smiled

vacantly.

He hated that damned smile. He averted his eyes. "It's about the murder of Mac's wife and child."

"Jay Copper ordered it and he's been arraigned for it."

"There's a hiccup."

"Sir?"

He leaned back in his chair with a grimace. "Copper has a nephew who he possibly sent along with Dan Jones on the hit." He also recalled that Copper had admitted to helping Peppy kill Dan Jones for his defection, not that they could prove it without that missing tape.

"I'm not surprised," she replied. "He has a lot of idiot relations. Most of them are doing hard time."

He glanced at her. "Bart Hancock isn't. And he's Harold Monroe's brother-in-law."

She was very still. The man had threatened her boss, but she hadn't connected him with the Kilraven case. "Bart Hancock."

"He's Jay Copper's nephew. His nickname is Peppy."

She let out a breath. "Oh, my God," she said, with reverence. She knew the name and the connection immediately, and it put another meaning on Monroe's warning that his family would get back at Jon Blackhawk.

If Peppy had killed a child . . .

"I can't talk to Mac about this, he'd go crazy," he told her. "And Winnie's very pregnant," he added, alluding to his sister-in-law's pregnancy.

"What are you going to do?" she asked.

"I don't know. Unless we can play connect-the-dots and find somebody, any-body, tied to the case who's willing to testify against him, I don't know what we can do. Most of the witnesses were killed, including Dan Jones and even his girlfriend."

"Her minister spoke to Dan Jones," she recalled at once.

"Yes, but he didn't actually speak to Dan Jones confidentially," he reminded her. "So he doesn't know anything. It's probably the only reason he's still alive."

She felt uneasy. "Harold Monroe wants revenge for his arrest."

He nodded. "He's a notorious fumbler."

"He's managed to avoid jail for the most part, until the kidnapping charge."

"Only because of Jay Copper, who's a master of intimidation," he replied. "But Copper's still in jail, awaiting trial, and even he can't do much intimidating from his present domicile. Not that he can't hire it done," he added heavily.

"Your brother has a friend in covert ops

who watched out for Winnie Sinclair's mother when she was in danger investigating the Kilraven murders," she reminded him. "Perhaps he could tag along with you."

He glared at her. "I'm a senior FBI agent," he reminded her coldly. "I do not require a bodyguard!"

She held up both hands. "No offense, but you can't watch your back all the time."

"Yes, I can."

She glowered at him. "There's the matter of kryptonite turning up in unusual places, Superman," she said with faint sarcasm.

"I didn't invite you in here to insult me," he pointed out.

"You wanted advice. I'm flattered that you value mine. Here it is. Don't tell your brother anything until you can find a witness who knows what Bart Hancock did — if he really was involved in the murder of Kilraven's family."

He sat back in the chair. It was a leather chair, old and not really cushy, but very comfortable. It was odd, she thought, for such a rigid, Spartan sort of man to like a comfortable chair at his desk when he provided hard chairs for visitors. But then, he was something of an anachronism himself.

"I suppose you're right," he replied quietly. Privately he was thinking how hard a job that was going to be, finding anybody connected to the case who was willing to risk his life to testify against a child murderer. Even civilians knew what happened to men who went to prison for that particular crime. They didn't last a long time incarcerated. The other inmates didn't appreciate child killers.

"You might involve Rick Marquez and Gail Sinclair," she advised, referring to two of the best homicide detectives on San Antonio's police force. "They're both familiar with the case, and Gail really is psychic. She might come up with some witness you haven't even considered."

He brightened a little. "That's good advice."

"Yes, it is," she mused, smiling.

He glared at her. "No reason to become conceited."

"But, sir, I have so much to be conceited about," she said haughtily. Her blue eyes twinkled. "Want to know what the stylists are doing for the holiday season this year? How about the latest fashion buzz from Paris?"

He was looking more irritable by the second. "When I want to know those things, I'll call Cammy and have her send her matrimonial prospect right over to enlighten me," he said sarcastically.

Her eyes widened. "I can call her for you. Right now, if you like."

"If you do, you'll really be out looking for a new job," he returned.

She shrugged. "Okay. But you don't know what you're missing. All those color predictions, skirt length changes . . ."

He stood up. "Out!" he said, pointing to the door.

She stood up, too. "Ingrate," she muttered.

He came around the desk. He was really tall, she thought, when he stopped less than an arm's length away from her. "You're a fountain of wisdom from time to time, Joceline," he said very softly. "We have our differences, but you're a real asset here."

She flushed. "Thanks."

He looked down into her eyes for longer than he meant to, and was suddenly aware of a new tension, a new electricity that arced between them.

Joceline felt her heart bounce up into her throat at the intensity of his gaze. She couldn't seem to tear her eyes away, and a huge shock surged up inside her like an almost tangible joy.

His eyes narrowed as he felt the same

impact of pleasure. His jaw tautened notice-ably.

"Your eyes are the oddest shade of blue I've ever seen," he remarked quietly. "Almost a royal blue."

"Yours are black," she replied, searching them.

"Yes." Involuntarily his lean, beautiful hand came up and touched her flushed cheek. "This is very dangerous," he said in a deep, velvety tone. "I might think of it as an invitation."

"I might point out that you're the one inviting trouble," she retorted and stepped back. There were reasons why she could never allow him closer than arm's length. "My legions of male admirers would set upon you like flies on honey and sunder you limb from limb. Not only that, there's this famous gorgeous movie star who calls me three times daily . . . and there he is, on the phone again!" she exclaimed, and almost ran from the office to answer the phone on her desk.

He was still laughing when he closed the door.

It had been a narrow escape. Joceline's knees were weak for the rest of the day every time she gazed at her gorgeous boss. She avoided looking directly at him, because she was afraid that he was right: she had been inviting trouble.

On the other hand, he'd touched her cheek. He was the one who'd come so very close to her. It was only the second time in their years together that he'd ever approached her in an intimate way — although it wasn't actually intimate. And he didn't remember the first time. She hoped, she prayed, that he never would.

An hour later, still dreaming of her boss, Joceline was feeding information into the computer when the part-timer, Phyllis Hicks, stopped by her desk with a question.

"These forms are so boring," she complained. "My dad works in the homicide department at San Antonio P.D. and I get to look at crime scene photos." Her eyes gleamed oddly. "Murder is such an exciting thing, don't you think?"

"Murder?"

Phyllis shifted. "The investigation, I mean. You get to catch criminals. My daddy's real good at it."

"Who is your dad?"

"His name's Dave Hicks, he works with Marquez." She made a face. "I don't like Marquez at all."

That was a surprise. Most people did.

Most women found him attractive.

"Of course, he's not my real dad," she added. "My real dad is special. He thinks outside the box. He's not afraid of anything." She laughed. "He lets me do stuff with him. It's very exciting." She caught herself and gave Joceline a beaming smile. "Sorry, I get carried away. Now about this form, do I have to fill in every single space?"

Joceline told her how to input the information, but long after Phyllis went back to her typing chores, Joceline sat quietly in her chair. She felt vaguely uneasy about the young woman. Was it normal to enjoy looking at crime scene photos? They made Joceline very ill. Once she'd even thrown up when she saw one in a file that involved the vicious killing of a young woman who'd threatened Senator Will Sanders. The woman had been brutally killed, a crime for which Jay Copper was charged. But Phyllis liked them?

There was no accounting for taste, she supposed, and there was the notorious forensic investigator, Alice Mayfield Jones Fowler, who really got into her work at crime scenes and never seemed to be bothered by what she had to see. On the other hand, Alice didn't find murder scenes exciting, either.

"I'll never fit in this modern society," Joceline muttered to herself. She didn't understand the fascination with death, with zombies, with vampires . . .

Well, she loved the very popular vampire movie trilogy, so that wasn't quite true. Perhaps Phyllis was just exaggerating. She might have never seen a crime scene photo. She was working in an office that dealt with violent crime, so perhaps she felt being excited by the process of crime-solving was expected.

Joceline shook her head and went back to work.

When quitting time came, she grabbed her purse, called good-night through the closed door and almost ran out of the building. She'd had enough for the day, after Phyllis's strange questions.

Even the fact that she had a worrisome meeting with school officials next was less disturbing than her boss's odd behavior. Joceline kept dark secrets. She had no wish to ever display them, least of all to Jon Blackhawk.

5

The head of the school, Mr. Morrison, and Markie's teacher, Ms. Rawles, were very nice about it. But they were emphatic that Markie's antics were disruptive and that he needed medication to prevent him from being a distraction to the other students.

Joceline just looked at them. She didn't agree or disagree.

"We would like your assurance that this matter will be resolved," Mr. Morrison said kindly. "Your pediatrician can put Markie on a medication to control his outbursts."

She smiled blankly. "In other words, you want me to go to my doctor and order him to put my four-year-old son on drugs?"

There were shocked, indignant looks.

She stood up, still smiling. "I'll have a long talk with my son. I'll also speak with our family physician. We don't have the funds to afford a pediatrician, I'm sorry to tell you. Markie's hospital visits are expensive, and we have an allergist in addition to a family physician, but we're rather limited in our budget. I have to have medical care for both of us, and a family practitioner is the best we can do right now."

They were still speechless.

"I will, however, speak with my family doctor about your insistence that Markie needs to become drug dependent. And if my physician agrees with you," she added sweetly, "then I will find another family physician."

"Uh, Mrs., that is, Miss, I mean Ms. Perry," Mr. Morrison stammered.

"I believe the politically correct designation is Ms.," she said helpfully.

"We only think Markie, being so young, requires some help with his difficulty in focusing . . ."

"That's right, sir, make sure that every child obeys without question so that teachers don't have to deal with any behavioral problems."

He glared at her. "Ms. Perry . . . !"

"In our defense," Ms. Rawles said gently, "our class has thirty-five students. We're much in the same boat as many other schools where teachers have to manage classrooms with thirty to forty students. We do the best we can. We really care about our students. But it's so hard to teach when we have children who simply can't pay attention. Markie is disruptive. He can't sit still, he talks out of turn, he gets into things . . ."

Joceline studied her. "Do you have children, Ms. Rawles?"

"I'm not married. I certainly wouldn't put the stigma of illegitimacy on my child," the other woman said at once, and then flushed, because she realized that Joceline had a child out of wedlock.

Joceline smiled, but she wasn't happy with the remark.

The principal cleared his throat. "I'm sure that whatever you and your physician decide will be fine with us."

"Of course," Ms. Rawles said, obviously distressed. "I'm very sorry. I never should have said such a thing to you!"

Their attitude took the edge off her temper. She could see their side of the issue, as well. "Actually Markie likes you very much, and so do I," Joceline cut her off. "It's all right. A lot of people have said worse things to me. His father was a very good man. We had too much to drink and did something out of character for both of us. He went missing in action overseas on duty before we could get married," she added gently, telling the falsehood with the confidence of

105

years of secret keeping.

The two school officials looked guilty.

"A tragedy," Ms. Rawles spoke for both of them. "The world is changing very quickly. Sometimes new concepts are difficult."

"I go to church, and take Markie, every Sunday," she told them with a quiet smile. "Everybody makes mistakes. Some are more difficult to live with than others. But I love my son. I feel blessed to have him."

They both brightened. "He's a smart little boy."

"That's why he's into everything, he's curious," Joceline replied. "And I have already discussed this with our doctor. He's researching medicines, but he says that discipline might be a better choice than drugs in Markie's case. I don't mean hitting him with a bat to get his attention," she added. "The doctor says that overactive children need consistency and routine and a limit to the number of toys they play with to keep them from being overstimulated. There are many new studies on both sides of the issue, but I would prefer to at least try the least drastic measure first. If it doesn't get results, then I'll have to consider other options. Compromise," she added with a smile, "is the foundation of civilization."

"It is," Mr. Morrison agreed, rising. He seemed to relax a little.

Ms. Rawles stood up, too. She smiled. "I apologize again for my remarks."

"It's all right," Joceline said again. "You'll let me know if the situation doesn't improve?" she asked the teacher.

Ms. Rawles nodded. "Yes, I will. And thank you for coming in to talk to us. I know your job requires long hours."

"Your job?" Mr. Morrison asked curiously.

"She works for the FBI," Ms. Rawles said with a grin, glancing at Mr. Morrison's shocked face.

"My goodness!" he blurted out. "I had no idea."

"I'm not involved in enforcement of federal laws," she said. "I only do the paperwork that helps get criminals convicted. I keep the gears oiled."

He chuckled. "How interesting! We're having a Career Day here in November. Perhaps you might like to speak about your duties?"

"I would," she said, "but my boss is very strict. He might not like it."

"We wouldn't want to get you in trouble with him," he replied. "But think about it."

"I will. Thank you both for being so understanding."

"I have two daughters in high school," Mr. Morrison said. "I do know how children can be." He was very quiet. "One of my daughters took Ritalin for ADD," he added, referring to attention deficit disorder.

Joceline wanted to ask, very badly, how that had turned out. But there was something in the man's face that deterred her. She thanked them again, said her goodbyes and went to pick up Markie at day care.

The next day she mentioned the principal's remark in passing to Agent Blackhawk.

"Morrison. Yes, the school principal. Sad story."

"Sir?"

"His eldest daughter is a senior in high school. She was arrested for possession of a Class I controlled substance and convicted of intent to distribute. She's on probation as a first offender. Her mother died of an overdose."

Joceline was shocked.

"You didn't hear that from me," he added. "We don't discuss cases brought by other agencies. In this case, San Antonio P.D."

"Yes, sir."

He cocked his head. "She was placed on drugs in grammar school for ADD."

"That would have been my next question until you said you wouldn't discuss it," she said demurely. She sighed. "They wanted me to get my doctor to put Markie on those drugs." She looked up quickly and grimaced. "That was uncalled for. I'm very sorry, sir. Personal matters should remain personal, especially on the job."

His black eyes were steady and quiet. "Are you going to do it?"

She moved uncomfortably. She didn't answer.

He moved closer. So close, in fact, that she could feel the heat of his powerful body and smell the spicy cologne he wore. She looked up at him and felt her heart jump.

"Are you going to do it?" he repeated, in a softer tone.

She swallowed. "I told them I'd talk to my family physician about giving Markie drugs for behavioral modification and that, if my family physician agreed, I'd get another family physician," she murmured dryly. "I didn't really mean it. I want to do what's best for Markie."

A chuckle escaped him. "I imagine that's not all you said."

Her blue eyes twinkled. "Well, Markie's teacher made a remark that hit me on the raw but I kept my cool. I can't help that everything I think appears on my face, though . . ."

He shook his head. "Ms. Perry, you are an anachronism."

"Sir?"

"It would take longer than I've got to explain," he replied, checking his watch. "I'm overdue for a meeting in the SAC's office."

"And I have work to do."

He pursed his lips. "Some people would consider making coffee 'work.' "

She smiled what he'd come to think of as her trademark expression. "Some people would consider a tomato a fruit."

"A tomato is a fruit."

She made a face and went back to her desk.

Markie wanted to play his video game. He grimaced when his mother started talking about his acting out in class and his inability to sit still.

"Nobody likes me," he muttered.

"Yes, they do. But when you won't stay at your desk, you make a lot of problems for your teacher. You aren't the only student she has."

He sighed. "It's so boring in there," he told her. "I already know all that stuff. But I'm younger than the other kids, and they make fun of me when I can't run like they can, on account of my lungs."

She felt that pain all the way to her shoes, but she knew from long and hard experience that bullies were a fact of life at any age. Unless the bullying was taking a dangerous toll, she found it best to let Markie handle those problems himself. Which he did. Once, when an older child tried to force him to give up his pocket money, he yelled "Thief!" at the top of his lungs until the owner came. He was reprimanded, but the bully got in trouble, too. He never tried to extort money again. For a sickly little boy, Joceline thought proudly, Markie had a stout and brave spirit. He wasn't afraid of anything.

"Why are you smiling?" he asked.

"I'm very proud of you," she said. "Your father would be proud of you, too, for the way you handle yourself when people try to pick on you."

"My dad was brave, wasn't he?"

"Very brave," she replied.

"Don't we have any pictures of him?" he asked.

This question was disturbing. She knew it would only get more difficult as time went by. "No, I don't," she said honestly. "I'm really sorry, Markie."

"Did he look like me?"

She studied him with a sad smile. "Only a little," she said, and hid her relief.

"Most of the other kids have daddies to take them places. I wish I knew him," he told her.

She picked him up and hugged him close. "I wish you did, too."

"You like your boss, don't you?" he asked when she put him down.

She felt flushed. "He's very nice."

"He plays video games just like us," he said.

"His brother plays them, too."

"You don't play much," he accused.

She bent and kissed his forehead. "I have housework to do. Mothers are busy people. But I play with you on the weekends, don't I?"

"Yeah. You do." He grinned at her. "And I beat you."

"Every time," she agreed with a laugh.

"I might let you win next time," he said thoughtfully.

"You might?"

He started to answer her playful reply when the phone rang.

Joceline picked up the receiver, still laughing from Markie's teasing. "Hello?"

There was a pause. It was cold and unnerving.

"Hello?" she asked again.

"Your boss is first," a gruff voice said. "Then you."

"What?" she exclaimed.

A dial tone was the only response she got. She wanted to think it was a mistake, a wrong number. But she knew it wasn't. She felt cold chills at the threatening words.

"Who was it, Mommy?"

"Just a wrong number, baby," she said, and forced a smile. "I have to get your clothes ready for school tomorrow. I'll be in the laundry room."

"Okay," he said absently, already lost in his video game.

Joceline closed the door of the playroom and leaned back against the wall with her eyes closed. She couldn't remember ever feeling so afraid.

She almost called her boss to tell him about the threat, but she thought she'd involved him too much already in her private life. It wasn't a good policy, to bring domestic problems to work. She didn't want to jeopardize his job, or her own. She didn't want him around Markie, either.

On the other hand, she had a sneaking hunch about the identity of her caller. She couldn't prove it. She'd only heard Harold Monroe's voice once, when he'd called brazenly to tell her boss he was out of jail. Strange, though, the voice seemed deeper than Monroe's. But he could be disguising it.

The call bothered her. So after she reminded Mr. Blackhawk about his day's schedule and noted that he had ten minutes free before he was due in federal court to testify on a case, she walked into his office and closed the door.

He gave her a surprised look.

She sat down in front of the desk. "I'm sorry, but I had a phone call last night, and although I can't swear to the identity of the caller, I think it might have been Harold Monroe."

He sat up straighter. His black eyes narrowed. "What did he say?"

"That you were first, and I was next."

His expression was hard to read. "Do you have an answering machine on your phone?"

She nodded enthusiastically. "Oh, yes, sir, and a ham radio and a plasma TV, a couple of sports cars . . . !"

"Ms. Perry," he said curtly.

"Sorry, sir. I forgot myself. Won't happen again." She crossed her heart.

He shook his head. "It's not a laughing matter."

"I wasn't laughing. It's just that I don't have the budget for that type of equipment," she said with a straight face.

"I should have known that."

Probably so, but, then, he and his brother — not to mention his seethingly rabid mother — were worth millions, if the gossip was true. She didn't doubt that he could walk into the nearest electronics store and purchase the highest-ticket item it contained without blinking an eye. Joceline was on a much stricter budget.

"You live in an unsecured apartment house," he said, thinking aloud.

"We have locks on the doors and a telephone."

He glared at her. "Locks keep honest people out. That's all they do."

She folded her hands in her lap. "Over the years that I've worked here," she began, "I've heard a lot of people make threats. I don't know of a single one that actually turned into an incident."

"Yes, well I do," he said curtly. "I won't take chances with your life, or your son's."

"It was your life I was thinking about," she said quietly. "He has a reason for wanting to harm you."

His eyebrows arched. "Are you actually expressing concern for my welfare, Ms.

Perry?" he asked with mock astonishment.

"Yes, sir," she said calmly. "It's very difficult to train a boss not to expect impossible menial tasks," she added with a gleam in her blue eyes. "I'm not anxious to break in somebody new."

He laughed faintly. "Touché." He glanced at his watch and got to his feet. "I'll talk to a few people and see what sort of arrangements I can make for someone to keep an eye on you after work."

"On our budget, sir, we can probably afford a ten-year-old boy in a trench coat with one of those Junior Spy kits."

He really glared at her then. "My brother has all sorts of shadowy contacts that we don't talk about. I'm sure at least one of them owes him a favor. Rourke comes to mind."

"No," she said at once. "No, absolutely not. I will not have that one-eyed lunatic anywhere near me!"

His eyebrows arched. She'd rarely been so outspoken about any of the people who came through the office. "He's very good at private security."

Her jaw set so tightly that it bulged.

"Out with it," he ordered.

She shifted restlessly. "He said I should be gagged and locked in a closet."

He had to stifle a laugh. "May I ask what prompted him to make such a remark?"

Her eyes avoided his. "He was making fun of my shoes."

He looked down. She was wearing the ballet slippers she usually wore to work, bad for the instep but extremely comfortable — and affordable.

"Some of us can't manage Neiman Marcus even on a good government salary," she said, still ruffled months after the remark was made.

"Rourke pops off and thinks he's being amusing."

"He'll get popped off if he makes another such remark to me," she said curtly.

He chuckled. "I'll see if anybody else owes Mac a favor."

"It sounded like Harold Monroe, but I couldn't prove it. He was probably just fishing, to see if he could frighten me. And he knew I'd tell you what he said," she added. She hesitated. "Sir, you really could use someone to watch your back. Monroe may be a certifiable idiot, but he has family connections who aren't."

"I'm aware of that."

"Don't get insulted," she added when he looked annoyed. "You FBI types always think you're the biggest, meanest dogs on the block and usually you're right. I don't like funerals," she added firmly.

"Or breaking in new bosses."

Her eyes twinkled. "Exactly."

"I'll do my best to stay alive." He started out the door and hesitated. "If my brother calls, tell him I want to talk to him. I'll be back after two."

"I did notice that, sir," she added pleasantly, "having noted it on your calendar."

His jaw clenched.

"Won't you be late for court?" she asked. "It's Judge Cummings sitting today, too, isn't it, and he doesn't like the FBI." She smiled angelically. "Do be polite, sir."

He muttered something under his breath.

"Sir!" she exclaimed. "This is a government office . . . !"

He was out the door before she could finish the sentence.

Betty Rimes was constantly amused by Joceline's ongoing verbal attacks on her boss.

"He could just fire you," Betty pointed out.

"He wouldn't dare. There are very few paralegals working outside the judicial system, where would he ever find someone to replace me?" Joceline asked, amused.

"We have a part-time administrative assistant," she was reminded grimly. "And Phyllis Hicks does offer to make coffee for the boss."

"I don't do menial chores," Joceline reiterated. "It isn't in my job description."

Betty sipped her coffee. "Yes, but, dear, she'd work for half what they pay you," she added worriedly. "It's a flat economy. So many people are out of work."

Joceline didn't let her uneasiness show. She just smiled. "Mr. Blackhawk is used to me and he doesn't like strangers."

"That's true. It's just that he doesn't make the major budgetary decisions."

Joceline stared at her. "What do you know that you're not telling me?"

Betty bit her lip. "It's probably nothing . . ."

"Tell me."

"I overheard one of the senior agents discussing something Mr. Grier said at lunch." Garon Grier was now the Special Agent in Charge for the Jacobsville satellite office, and he frequently showed up at the San Antonio office to have lunch with the San Antonio SAC. "Mr. Grier was disturbed at talk that they were going to reduce his office staff, and our own SAC apparently wondered out loud if we could make do

119

with one administrative assistant for the Violent Crimes Squad here, with a part-time assistant."

Joceline didn't move. She stared at the other woman with dawning horror. Betty had been with the Bureau for a long time, over ten years, and she had seniority.

"I said it was probably just talk. He might have even been joking. Please don't worry," Betty said gently. "Probably they'll come up with some other idea for saving money by cutting our travel budget. I just didn't want it to come at you out of the blue. You're a great paralegal. I know Judge Cummings would snap you up in a second for his office, or the assistant D.A. would for hers."

That was true. But no matter how good the working conditions, or how great the pay, those offices wouldn't contain Jon Blackhawk. While that might be a good thing, in some respects, it was devastating in another.

"Joceline, you're not going to lose your job," Betty said, her tone reassuring. "The SAC and Mr. Blackhawk would both fight for you."

They would. She knew that. Despite her insistence on the parameters of her duties, she was good at what she did, and she never slacked or avoided work. There were those unavoidable times when she was late for work . . .

She looked up at Betty worriedly. "I've been late sometimes."

The older woman was sympathetic. "Everybody knows why," she said surprisingly.

"What?"

"We know your son has medical problems," the older woman replied with a smile.

"But I never told anyone," she stammered. "I mean, Mr. Blackhawk came by when I had to bring Markie to the hospital," she began.

"And he told all of us," she said. "He didn't want anyone assuming that you missed work for some frivolous reason. He's quite fond of you, in his way. Although watching him react to you is funny. You do put his back up, as they say."

"Keeps him on his toes." Joceline laughed. "He really does tend to brood."

"Oh, coffee!" Phyllis said, smiling. "Can I have some, too?"

"Sure, sit down," Joceline invited. She noted the younger woman's clothing; it looked like the sort of thing Cammy Blackhawk would wear. But Phyllis had said her father worked as a police detective and Phyllis was in college part-time. Where would she get the money for expensive clothes? Maybe Joceline was just tired and getting irritated over minor matters.

"We were talking about our workload," Betty commented.

"It's so boring," Phyllis said. "I wish I could be a detective, like my dad, and get to go to crime scenes."

"You watch too many crime television shows, Phyllis." Betty chuckled.

Phyllis gave her a blank stare.

"You know, those forensic programs that deal with trace evidence solving big cases," Joceline said helpfully. "They call it fiction."

"So many people don't know the difference." Betty sighed. "Now juries are so clued up that they argue with attorneys about trace evidence in murder trials. They watch a television show a few times and think they're qualified to rule on pathological evidence."

"Yes, it's nothing like what they show on television," Phyllis said. "Bodies are so clean and tidy. In real life, the blood is everywhere. It splashes around like paint . . ." She stopped because they were staring at her silently. "Oh, my dad lets me look at file photos sometimes," she said quickly. "To teach me how evidence is really gathered."

"I see," Betty said, but she was visibly uncomfortable.

"Some of those shows are just a little too graphic for me, especially when my son might walk in and see something that would give him nightmares," Joceline said with a smile.

"I was never squeamish, even when I was little," Phyllis scoffed. "That murder case we worked on with Mr. Blackhawk was really fascinating, the one that Jay Copper got arrested for," she added suddenly. "Aren't you working with a file about that Hancock man? Digging out information about his past?"

"I'm trying to run down stuff. I got some rap sheets from San Antonio P.D. this morning. They're on my desk. I haven't had time to input the information. I may have to sign them out and do it at home."

"I guess it's a long rap sheet," Phyllis said.

"Very."

"Such a sad case, the Kilraven murders," Betty said. "Imagine, someone killing a child like that."

"Kids, adults, a life is a life." Phyllis shrugged. "They all die the same."

"You have a different outlook when you have a child," Joceline said tautly.

Phyllis assumed a smile. "Well, of course you do."

Betty sipped more coffee. "I worry about

Monroe's threats," she said somberly. "Mr. Blackhawk seems to think it's a joke, but the man is dangerous. His wife's uncle taught him how to be a monster, and his brother-in-law is a terror."

Joceline nodded. "Jay Copper is going to do some very hard time, if he manages to avoid the needle," she added meaningfully. "Imagine ordering the death of a woman and a small child!"

"And I'm sure that he did order it, despite all his denials," Betty said grimly. "Dan Jones may have done the actual killing, but Jay Copper was behind it. If they can just convict him, is the thing. I hope they do."

"Mr. Blackhawk is supposed to meet an informant tonight at seven," Joceline said heavily. "He refuses to have a bodyguard. He doesn't think Monroe is a threat."

"That's foolhardy," Betty said. "Look what happened to Detective Marquez when he went to meet some shadowy informant."

Marquez had been blindsided and hospitalized. Joceline was uneasy about the meeting tonight. "Mr. Blackhawk takes chances."

"Oh, I'm sure he'll be all right," Phyllis said airily. She glanced at her watch — a very expensive one. "Gosh, I have to get back to work. Thanks for the coffee."

She left without putting change in the

kitty that helped pay for renewing the canteen supplies. Without a word, Betty took a bill out of her pocket and placed it in the container.

"Young people." She sighed.

Joceline smiled. "You're nice."

"Thanks. So are you."

"I do hope they can convict Jay Copper of little Melly Kilraven's murder," Joceline said quietly. "Kilraven still isn't over it," she added gently, "although he and his wife, Winnie, are expecting around the new year." She smiled. "What a Christmas present they're going to have this year if she goes into labor early!"

"Christmas!" Betty exclaimed. "I haven't even started shopping!"

"It isn't even Thanksgiving yet," she was reminded.

"Yes, but I usually have everything bought by August." She laughed. "I'm efficient on the job. I wish I could be that efficient off it."

Joceline laughed, too. "Well, we all do what we can."

The phone rang. Joceline got to her feet. "Back to work. Thanks for the heads-up," she added in a soft tone. "At least if I get the ax, I'll be somewhat prepared. Perhaps I should start working up a résumé."

"Wait," Betty advised. "A lot of this is all talk. I don't think the office can operate with just me taking a workload from the squad, and only a part-timer for Mr. Blackhawk all at once. I'd have a nervous breakdown. And I can't persuade people to talk to me like you can. You're marvelous at digging out information."

Joceline pursed her lips. "I can do that," she agreed. "Maybe there's work for a skip tracer," she added, indicating a line of work that involved digging out information for detectives. "I might look good in a trench coat."

Betty laughed again.

Just before quitting time, the phone rang as Joceline was gathering things into her bag to take home, including the long file on Bart Hancock.

Joceline picked up the phone. "Hello?"

"My love! It's been so long!"

She knew that voice. Its South African accent was unmistakable. She pictured a rugged, tanned face with an eye patch and blond hair in a long ponytail. "Rourke," she muttered.

"You know you're happy to have me around again," he drawled. "Guess what? I'm going to be your shadow for a few weeks. Until the would-be perp stops making threats, at least."

"I can't wait," she replied. "Do you have body armor?"

He hesitated. "Excuse me?"

"Body armor," she emphasized. "Riot gear."

"No. But I can borrow some. Why will I need it?"

"If you attempt to shadow me, I'll rub bear grease all over you and open the lion cage at the zoo," she said sweetly.

There was a slow, deep chuckle. "Joceline, my love, I have two tame lions who live with me back home in South Africa. I'm not intimidated by big cats. However, if you'd like to rub me all over with bear grease," he added in a deep, velvety tone, "I can be in your office in two minutes flat. I'll even run red lights!"

She slammed the receiver down, her lips making a thin line. She muttered under her breath.

A minute later, the phone rang again. She jerked it up and, without thinking, said, "If you call here one more time, Rourke, I'll have you up for harassment!"

There was a faint pause, as if she'd shocked the listener. Then Kilraven's voice came over the line, deep and very somber.

"Joceline, I've got some bad news."

"Winnie . . . ?" she began worriedly, because she was fond of his wife. They often went shopping together.

He swallowed. "Not Winnie. My brother . . ."

"Jon? Something's happened to Jon?" She sounded almost hysterical and she didn't care. Harold Monroe's phone call came back to her in a flash of anguish. She gripped the phone, hard. "What happened?"

"He's been shot. Critically. He's at the Hal Marshall Memorial Medical Center . . . Hello? Joceline?"

He was talking to himself. Joceline had her purse over her shoulder. She ran to Betty's small office and told her what had happened.

"I'm on my way to the hospital. I'll call you the minute I know something!"

Betty started to mention that Jon's family was certainly gathered around him, and would relay any news. But the look on Joceline's face stopped the words in her mouth. She wondered if Joceline was even aware of her feelings for Jon Blackhawk, which were blatant on her drawn, worried face.

6

Kilraven was sitting in an uncomfortable chair in the emergency room waiting area, with Winnie beside him. He looked up when Joceline walked in. His expression, usually unreadable, was as concerned as hers.

"Have you heard anything new?" she asked, pausing to greet Winnie with a hug.

"They've taken him into surgery," Kilraven replied grimly. "They said they'll know more when they operate. He was shot in the back. In the back!"

Joceline's face flamed. "I hope they find Harold Monroe and hang him."

Kilraven nodded. "I can't prove it, but I'm sure he's the one who did it. And I'll find the proof, no matter how long it takes me!"

"I'll help," Joceline agreed harshly.

"Want some coffee?" Winnie asked her husband, who nodded.

"I'll go get it," he said, starting to rise.

She pushed him back down. "I need the

exercise. The doctor says it's good for me to move around. But thanks, sweetheart." She bent to kiss him. "Would you like a cup, Joceline?" she added.

"Yes, please." Joceline dug for a dollar bill and handed it to her insistently. "You're not buying me coffee," she said stubbornly. "I'm an employee of a federal agency and I won't be the subject of a bribery scandal," she added with mock hauteur.

Winnie chuckled. "Have it your way, Elliott Ness."

Kilraven frowned. "He headed up the FBI in Chicago during racketeering days. He was incorruptible."

"The history professor," Winnie teased, and kissed him again.

"I'm not up on American history unless it has Scots connections." His area of expertise was seventeenth-century Scottish history.

"Was Elliott Ness a Scot?" Joceline wondered aloud.

"I'll look into it," Kilraven promised.

Winnie went to get coffee. Kilraven and Joceline sat rigidly, watching the doors open and close as medical personnel in green scrubs went to and fro, occasionally flanked by white-coated physicians with stethoscopes draped around their necks.

"Busy place," Kilraven ventured.

"Yes." She turned over her purse. "Have you called your mother?"

"She's on her way here," he said. "I made her promise not to drive." He grimaced. "She's wrapped two cars around telephone poles in the past five years."

"Oh. She drives like you, then," Joceline said with a pleasant smile.

He glared at her. "I have never wrecked a car."

"Sorry. I forgot. They were blown out from under you. Major difference." She was nodding.

He shifted. "Everybody gets bomb threats."

"Yours aren't threats, and how lucky that you weren't in the cars at the time they exploded."

"Can I help it if I inspire passion in people?"

"People in black ops do that, I'm told." She chuckled.

He shrugged. "I'm trying to walk the straight and narrow, especially now," he said with a smile. "I'm doing the most boring job the company could find for me. Surveillance."

"It's safer than what you used to do," she said. She frowned. "Did you send Rourke after me?"

"Yes, I did," he said, "and stop trying to run him off. Monroe is deadly serious, as you might have noticed today. Jon told me that Monroe said you're next. You have a small child and the two of you live in an apartment building with no security to speak of. Rourke will protect you."

"Who's going to protect him from me?" she wondered aloud.

"That is a good question."

They paused to stare at the door leading to the surgical wing. A surgeon in green scrubs came out it, looked toward Kilraven and motioned for him to join him. Joceline went, too, ignoring the surgeon's obvious surprise. Under other circumstances, Kilraven would have chuckled at her concern for a boss she constantly drove nuts.

Joceline could hear her own heart beating and hoped Kilraven wouldn't notice. She was scared to death. If Jon Blackhawk died, it would be like the sun going out forever. She refused to even entertain the possibility. But she knew that he could die. And might. She gripped her purse like a lifeline, hoping, praying . . . *let him live, please, I'll go to church more, I'll give to charity more, I'll be a better person, be kinder, more tolerant . . .* She closed her eyes. *You can't bargain with God,* she told herself.

"I'm cautiously optimistic," the surgeon said, glancing at Joceline when her explosion of soft breath diverted him. "The bullet missed the major organs and lodged in the wall of his chest. It did some damage to a lung, and of course filled the pleural cavity with blood. We've removed the bullet and inserted a tube to drain the excess fluid and reinflate the lung. The damage to his lung is minimal. Apparently he was shot from a distance, and with a nonfragmenting bullet, thank God. The damage will heal. It helps that he's young and in great physical shape."

"Can I see him?" Kilraven asked quietly.

He hesitated. But he was a kindly man, and these two people loved his patient. He wondered if the woman was a girlfriend. She was certainly concerned.

"In a few minutes," he told them. "We'll move him into recovery temporarily, then he'll go to ICU for a day or two. Just as a precaution," he emphasized when he noted his two listeners going pale. "We want to make sure complications don't develop that might retard his progress. We'll keep him for three or four days after that, again, to make sure he's progressing as we think he should. But I think he'll be fine," he added gently.

"They'll come to get us, when we can see him?" Kilraven asked, glancing at Joceline as if it were a given that she'd go in, too.

"I'll send a nurse," he promised. "He's an FBI agent, isn't he?"

"Yes," Kilraven replied. "One of the best."

"We do a big business in gunshot wounds in our emergency room," the doctor said with a heavy sigh. "Sadly there are more guns than trauma surgeons in this area."

"One day that will change," Kilraven said.

The doctor only smiled. "Not in my lifetime, I'm afraid. I'll get back to work. They just brought in a child of seven, victim of a drive-by shooting." He shook his head. "In my day, drugs were only whispered about. There was no wide-scale distribution, no gangs with guns, no . . ." He shrugged. "It was a less tolerant world, but far less violent."

"They did this experiment," Kilraven said quietly. "I read about it. They put rats in a confined area until they were so crowded that they could barely move. They became aggressive and began attacking the others and even cannibalizing them."

The doctor nodded. "We are too many, with too few resources, in too little space in cities on this planet. Nature has a way of thinning the population without any help from us." He glanced toward the emergency room. "However, I must add that I prefer nature's approach. Guns and knives are messy."

"I agree," Kilraven said. "I've seen my share of the results."

Nobody added that he'd helped a few criminals into emergency rooms.

The surgeon smiled reassuringly and went back to work.

Joceline was trying to avoid letting Kilraven see her tears.

"Hey, now," he said in a teasing tone. "Don't do that. Never let them see you cry."

She laughed with a hiccup and brushed at her eyes. "He's an awful boss," she muttered. "Keeps me working late, throws things, insults me . . ."

"Jon insults you?" he asked, shocked.

"He asks me to make coffee," she scoffed. She brushed away another tear. "Imagine that!"

"He's just tired of threatened lawsuits from visiting attorneys who have to drink the coffee the agents make," Kilraven explained.

"Then they should stop letting Murdock make coffee," she pointed out.

"That's been suggested," he replied. "At the same time, they mentioned dirt and shovels . . ."

"There's a large potted plant in our office that could use a jolt of fertilizer," she mused. "However, Agent Murdock is far too large to plant in it."

"We could . . ." he began enthusiastically.

She held up a hand and glowered at him. "Please! This is a hospital!"

"Just a thought." He sighed. "I bring my own coffee now when I visit Jon at his office, though."

At the sound of her boss's name, she relaxed a little. "I'm glad he'll be all right." She hesitated. "I guess I should get going."

"You can see him first."

She was uncertain. "You and Winnie should go in."

"Winnie will say that you should," he said with a gentle smile.

"Thanks," she murmured huskily and wouldn't look up.

Kilraven didn't say what he was thinking. Joceline and Jon had been antagonistic toward each other for a long time. But there was one night when they'd actually gone to a party together, about four years ago. The Bureau had been providing protection for a young woman who was dating a foreign dignitary's son, and avoided a kidnapping. She'd insisted that Jon, the agent in charge of the case, come to her birthday party and bring a date. So Jon had made Joceline go with him. He hated parties. He hated socializing. So did Joceline. But she went.

Funny, Joceline had acted oddly afterward and tried to quit her job. Jon had talked her into staying. He hadn't said much about the incident, just that he'd had way too much to drink and Joceline had been forced to drive him to the hospital. It turned out that someone had spiked Jon's drink with a hallucinogenic drug, trying to be funny. The culprit, a foreign dignitary's son, had fled the country shortly thereafter and never returned.

He hadn't thought about that for a long time. His brother never drank as a rule. He was very straitlaced. Today, it had hurt terribly to see Jon lying on a gurney with blood seeping from the wound on his back. He loved his brother. Cammy was going to go ballistic. She'd lived in fear of this all during Jon's career in law enforcement. She kept rosaries everywhere, even in the glove compartment of her car, and she prayed constantly for his safety. At least she wasn't driving herself to the hospital or there might be two tragedies. Kilraven would have gone to get her, but he'd been afraid to leave Jon — as if by his own physical presence he could keep Jon alive.

The nurse beckoned to them a nerve-racking few minutes later. Neither Kilraven nor Joceline really believed that Jon wasn't going to die. They had to see him for themselves, to be sure.

He was in a hospital gown, but his chest was bare. He was white as a sheet. There was dried blood on his firm, chiseled mouth. He was laboring to breathe, even with the tube that ran out of his chest to drain off the fluid. There was a drip feeding from a tube on a pole into his arm. There were oxygen tubes in his nostrils and he was hooked up to half a dozen monitors. His long, jet-black hair was tangled on the pillow. His eyes were closed.

Besides the beep of the monitors and the electronic sounds, there was only the sudden jerk of Joceline's breath, almost a sob, which she quickly smothered.

"He'd hate having his hair tangled," she said quietly.

"Yes."

He glanced at her, noting that she didn't have much more color in her face than Jon did in his. She was gripping her purse as if she feared it might escape.

"He's one tough customer," Kilraven told her comfortingly. "And I do know something about gunshot wounds. I'm sure he's in a lot of pain, and it will take time for him to recover. But he's going to live, Joceline."

She swallowed her fear and nodded slowly. "Yes," she agreed.

"Tomorrow he'll be telling the nurses how to do the drip and threatening the doctor to try to get out of the hospital."

She nodded again. It was so painful to see him like that. He was such a strong, vital man . . .

Kilraven was watching her covertly. It surprised him to see her at a loss for words, to see her so frightened. Perhaps she was thinking about the shadowy man in her life who went missing overseas. Markie's father.

Markie. He felt a sudden sinking worry. "Going to step out for just a sec," he told her, and moved out of the ICU unit to make a quick phone call.

Joceline barely noticed. Her hand went out to smooth the thick, long, tangled black hair on the pillow. She recalled another time when she'd touched it, felt its cool silkiness, clung to it as feelings rose so high that she thought she might die of them. He didn't remember. It was a good thing. She didn't want him to remember.

"Don't touch my son!"

She froze, jerking her hand back, as

139

Cammy Blackhawk came into the room. She glared at the younger woman as she moved to the bed, her back to Joceline.

"Jon," she whispered. "My poor, poor boy!"

She bent to kiss his forehead, and fought tears. She smoothed back his hair and stared at him for a long moment. Then she turned to Joceline, all cold dignity and hostility.

"You have no right to be in here," she snapped.

Joceline didn't argue. She looked one last time at Jon before she turned and left the cubicle.

"Where are you going?" Kilraven asked, surprised to meet her in the hall.

"I'm leaving," Joceline said, very pale but composed. "Life goes on. Your mother is in there," she added stiffly.

"Oh, God, now the real torment begins," he groaned. "She'll stand the staff on its ear and they'll threaten to hang her from a window by a sheet!"

She laughed suddenly.

"Don't let her worry you," Kilraven said in a low tone. "She's not what she seems. Honest."

Joceline didn't reply. "I hope he does well."

"He will. I'll call you myself if there's any change."

She nodded. "Thanks, Kilraven."

His eyes narrowed. "Joceline, I've had Rourke stake out your son's preschool."

"What?" she exclaimed, going white.

"Monroe made threats," he reminded her. "We can't prove it so we can't have him arrested. He's being watched, that's all I can say. But your son may be on the firing line. He has to have protection. So do you."

It was horrifying to think that Markie might end up in a hospital bed, victim of some deranged criminal. "Surely, not! He's just a child!"

"So was Melly," Kilraven reminded her with a grim expression, speaking of his daughter who had been killed. "She was barely three, when —" His voice broke.

"I'm sorry," she told him. "Truly sorry."

"Sorry doesn't bring her back, and it won't protect your son, either," he added. "Rourke will. So tolerate him."

She grimaced.

"You don't have to like him. I know he's a pain. But he's the best private security I know."

"All right."

He studied her for a moment. "You never bring your son to work. You don't have a

141

photo of him on your desk. But you obviously love him very much."

"Don't speculate," she bit off.

He was just staring at her. Not even blinking. "I'm not speculating."

"I keep my work life and my home life separate," she said stiffly. "I'm somewhat defensive about my status," she added, and averted her eyes.

"So you don't draw attention to it."

"Yes," she said quickly, anxious for an answer that would shut him up.

"I get it." He didn't press her. But he was getting some very interesting vibrations running underneath the casual conversation. "Don't worry about your boss," he added gently. "He's in great hands."

She looked toward the glass cubicle, where Cammy Blackhawk was still smoothing her son's hair and talking to him. "I noticed."

"I meant the doctor," he mused.

"Oh."

"You don't know about Cammy's past, and I won't tell it to you," he said surprisingly. "But there's a reason she's the way she is. Try not to take her attitude too seriously."

"She loves her son. There's nothing wrong with that."

"She does, but she's micromanaging his

life. Or she's trying to."

"She wants the best for him." She pursed her lips and her blue eyes twinkled suddenly. "She wants him to have the best fashion advice money can buy."

"He'd do a lot better with a woman who could play video games with him."

"Don't look at me," Joceline said firmly. "I have one man in my life. I don't need another."

"Your son's father went missing in action, you said."

"Yes."

"I still have contacts in active military circles," he said, watching her with uncanny closeness. "I could have them do some checking."

She dropped her purse. She bent and picked it up. "Sorry, it's been an unsettling day," she said. "I'm clumsy. No, thanks, it's already been checked out. He disappeared in those mountains where they think the remnants of Al-Qaeda were hiding in a secret base. They were certain that he was killed, they just were reluctant to tell me."

She hadn't looked up once.

"I see," he said.

She was hoping for an interruption when Winnie Sinclair came up with two cups of coffee. She handed one to her husband.

"You've had a long day, you should go."

"Yes," Joceline said gratefully. "You'll call me, if there's any change?" she added worriedly.

"Of course we will," Winnie assured her.

"The assistant D.A. asked about you," Kilraven said. "She's still hoping you might jump ship and go to work for her," he added, teasing.

"There might be a real possibility of that," Joceline said on a heavy sigh. "They're talking about cutting staff in my office. Betty has seniority, so if one of us is cut, it will be me." She shook her head. "This has been a bummer of a day."

Kilraven frowned. "They'd never let you go."

She smiled sadly. "They'll let anybody go, if they have to. I don't have any illusions about being the best administrative assistant on earth." She sighed. "Now I have to worry about that and my boss, and my son . . ."

"Not about Markie," Kilraven assured her. "Rourke will make sure no harm comes to him. Or to you."

Joceline ground her teeth together. "Okay."

"And Jon will be all right," he added.

She bit her lip. "He had blood on his mouth."

"Joceline, he was shot in a lung," he reminded her. "He would have been spitting up blood when they found him. Thank God he was in sight of a main street when it happened!"

"Yes," she whispered, hurting as she considered how frightening and how painful it would have been, to have experienced what her boss had — to be shot in the back.

"Now go home to your son," Winnie said gently. "He will keep you from brooding too much."

"The chief brooder is in there." She indicated the cubicle where Cammy was still sitting with Jon. "He does it much better than I do."

"He'll be fine. Just keep the office together until he recovers," Kilraven told her.

She smiled. That was optimistic. She had to be optimistic, too. "Okay. Do you know any really good defense attorneys, by the way?"

Kilraven blinked. "Not really, but I can ask around. Why do you need one?"

"I don't, yet. As long as Rourke stays out of sight."

Kilraven chuckled. "He is a piece of work, isn't he?"

"Saved your butt, my darling," Winnie reminded him with a hug.

He returned it and kissed her hair. "Yes, but he was being obnoxious."

"It's what he does best."

"He'll keep Markie safe," Kilraven reminded Joceline. "He's good at what he does."

"Which would be what, exactly, when he isn't returning favors for you?" Joceline asked curiously.

"Never you mind," he said firmly. "That's need to know, and you don't."

"Spoilsport."

She smiled at both of them and sent one last, worried glance toward where Jon Blackhawk lay, so quiet and still, before she left the waiting room.

"Something's fishy," Kilraven murmured.

"About what?" Winnie asked.

He didn't tell her. He had his suspicions, all wrapped up in mystery and Joceline's reticence. But he was going to do some digging, when he had time.

He and Winnie went back to ICU to join Cammy.

"Has she gone, that awful girl?" Cammy asked angrily.

"She's his right arm at work," Kilraven reminded her firmly. "She's stood by him when half a dozen other women would have run screaming out the door."

"I don't like her. She's not a moral person."

"What if she'd ended the pregnancy, would that make her any more moral in your eyes, Cammy?" Kilraven asked coldly. "What if it had been you, pregnant with Jon?"

Cammy swallowed, hard, and averted her eyes. Her jaw tightened. He was provoking nightmares and she couldn't even tell him. She couldn't tell anyone. She smoothed Jon's hair. "He looks so pale."

"His system has been through a shock," Kilraven reminded her. "Been there, done that."

"Yes, I know, my dear," she said gently, and she hugged him. "I'm sorry. I'm being terrible. I was so worried . . ." Tears stung her eyes.

He hugged her. "Jon's going to be fine."

"Yes."

He sighed. "I thought the murders were neatly wrapped up. But there's a new trail emerging. I just found out that the guy we think did this," he indicated Jon, "has a brother-in-law who may also have been involved in Melly's death."

"What?" Cammy exclaimed, horrified.

"That's not all. Now he's after Joceline's little boy." He wasn't certain of that, but it

147

was a good guess.

Cammy was conflicted. She didn't like that Joceline person. But she loved children. Anybody's children. "That's too bad."

"It is."

"She doesn't have a live-in boyfriend or someone who could protect him?"

"Joceline lives alone. But I sent Rourke to watch the boy."

"Rourke." She rolled her eyes. "Well, on the other hand, he is a bachelor and of an age to marry." She was thoughtful. If Joceline married Rourke, she'd move to South Africa, far from Jon. She smiled. "Perhaps they might like each other."

Kilraven didn't reply. He could see wheels turning in Cammy's mind, and suddenly he felt sorry for Rourke.

Joceline dropped her things off at her apartment. She was going to be late getting Markie, but she'd phoned and the owner, especially under the circumstances, told her to take her time that she'd be glad to wait. She'd heard about Jon's shooting on the news. She was very sorry. Not nearly as sorry as Joceline, who was sick and worried out of her mind.

If he died, how would she live with the secret she kept? It gnawed at her like a dog

148

with a bone. She was so upset that her hands shook as she locked her door and went out to get into her car. She thought she saw a shadow move, but she was certain it was her imagination. She was so much on edge, she was seeing things.

She tried to put Jon's condition in the back of her mind. She didn't want to upset Markie. She thanked the owner profusely when she picked up Markie at the day care center. He had new drawings to show her. "This is my teacher," he said, showing her a sketch he'd done, which was crude but recognizable. "And this is a dog that came to the playground. A man came in a truck and took him away," he added sadly. "Will they kill him?"

"No! They'll just find his owner. That's all." She smiled and hoped that it was the truth.

"I wish we could have a dog," he said.

She fastened him into the backseat and got in behind the steering wheel. Of all the things about modern life that she disliked, this was her pet peeve. A child should sit beside its parent, not isolated in the backseat. Yes, air bags saved lives and they were dangerous and could kill a small child. But when she had been small, Joceline had ridden in the front seat of her father's pickup truck, strapped in like a miniature adult, happy and laughing. Someone should figure out a child seat that could withstand the air bags going off, and allow kids to be closer to their parents.

She sighed as she pulled out into traffic. Her boss was going to be all right. He was going to be all right. She had to believe that, to save her own sanity. Markie would be all right, too. Rourke would watch out for him. She didn't have to like Rourke to know that he was good at his job — whatever it was, when he wasn't doing favors for Kilraven. She started looking around to see if she could recognize the one-eyed lunatic in any passing cars.

"Mommy, are you looking for somebody?" Markie asked curiously.

She cleared her throat. "I'm just checking traffic, that's all."

"Isn't your boss named Mr. Blackhawk? Somebody said he was shot. Is he dead?"

"No! He's just wounded and in the hospital. He's not dead," she said at once.

"I'm glad. We played video games with him that night. I like him."

She smiled sadly. "I like him, too."

"Could we go and see him?" he asked.

Joceline, surprised, just stammered. "There's an age limit, Markie," she foundered. Well, there used to be. She wasn't sure of modern hospital policy. It had been several years since she herself had been in one, when she'd had Markie.

"You mean I can't see him?"

"Yes. That's what I mean. His mother is with him."

"Oh, that's okay, then."

Joceline had other thoughts about that, but she didn't share them. "How about an ice-cream cone?" she asked.

"Wow! Could we?"

"Yes." It was the little things, she considered, that made life bearable. Even the hard times were smoothed over by something simple and comforting.

She stopped at an ice-cream parlor and ordered two cones, strawberry for herself and butter pecan for Markie. She handed his to him with a smile.

He licked it and laughed up at her with sparkling eyes. He was going to be handsome when he was older, she thought. She thanked God every day that he looked more like her than his father.

When they got home, just after dark, the front door was standing open.

"Stay here," Joceline told Markie firmly.

"What is it, Mommy?"

She didn't answer. She went to a point

where she could see the front door. Nothing was visible inside it. She knew better than to walk into the apartment. Someone had broken in. Someone who might still be in there, might be armed, might want to kill Joceline and Markie just for their closeness to Jon Blackhawk . . . !

"Well!" came a deeply accented voice from inside the apartment. "It's a good thing you didn't come home sooner."

And Rourke appeared in the doorway, big and handsome and smiling.

7

"Rourke!" Joceline exclaimed. "You idiot! You scared me to death!"

He strode down the steps, his hands in his pockets, whistling. He was tall and lean and muscular, with long blond hair in a ponytail down his back. He had one light brown eye. The other was hidden under a rakish black eye patch. "Now, darlin', if I hadn't come along when I did, you'd have had a very bad shock when you opened that front door. Hi, little feller. How are you?" he asked the small boy in the backseat in a very pronounced South African accent.

"I'm good," Markie said. "Who are you?"

"Rourke," was the amused reply.

"You only got one eye."

"I noticed," Rourke told him, not taking offense.

"I'm sorry."

The man looked at the boy with a visible softening. "Nice of you to say that."

"Did some mean man hurt you?"

"You might say that," Rourke replied.

"I like your eye patch. You could be a pirate on Halloween."

Rourke burst out laughing. "You know, I've been called a pirate a time or two." He looked pointedly at Joceline.

"Why are you here, and what's wrong with the apartment?" she asked worriedly.

"Nothing major. Step over here a bit." He smiled reassuringly at Markie. But when he turned back to Joceline, his hard face was solemn. "Someone had a go at your desk. At a guess, they were looking for something. Any idea what?"

Her heart stopped. She had no important papers, nothing that would interest an outsider. There was only the usual things, bank deposit records, tax information, Markie's birth certificate and her own, nothing . . . nothing . . . There was her diary!

She brushed past Rourke and ran into the apartment in a panic. She kept the diary in her bedside table, but it was under a mass of other objects, like paperbacks and a pad and pen, over-the-counter analgesics, booklets and instructions for electronic things like her clock. She fumbled in the drawer, horrified at some of the things she'd written down. It had never occurred to her that anyone would rob her!

She pulled out books, scattering them, scared to death. But then, there it was, at the bottom of the drawer, its small lock intact. It hadn't been opened. She clutched it to her breast and shivered with reaction.

"Something damaging in there, I presume?" Rourke asked gently.

She looked at him with sick fear. "People write things that they never should."

He nodded solemnly. "Yes."

She drew in a harsh breath. "I'd better burn it, I think."

"Put it in the bank, in a safe-deposit box," he suggested.

She stared at him. "Along with my diamond collection and my gold bars."

He laughed.

"Listen, I can barely pay the rent. There's no money for extras. It's better to destroy it. No good could come of keeping it, anyway."

"Keeping what, Mommy?" Markie asked as he joined them. Rourke had brought him inside the minute Joceline vanished into the apartment.

She grimaced at her lack of instinct, leaving Markie alone in the car.

"It's all right, I've got your back," Rourke assured her with a smile.

"It's just a diary, Markie," Joceline told him. "I wanted to make sure I knew where it was, that's all."

"Can I read it?"

She swallowed. "When you're older."

"Okay."

Rourke was watching her through a narrowed pale brown eye. Something in that diary was enough to make her panic. He wondered what it was.

The rest of the apartment was seemingly untouched, at first glance. Joceline was nervous. Someone had touched her things, invaded her privacy. She felt violated. Now she wondered if she needed new locks.

"Yes, you do," Rourke said when she mentioned it. "I'll install dead bolts tomorrow. Do you need permission from the landlord?"

She shook her head. "I asked once before and the manager approved it, in writing. I just didn't get around to it."

Rourke nodded.

Her expression was briefly unguarded as she looked up at him. "I wasn't scared before," she said unsteadily.

His one eye narrowed, and his lean face hardened. "Any normal human being would be afraid for a child," he said quietly, so that Markie didn't hear.

She turned on the small television. "Time for someone's favorite show, I believe?" she teased, putting Markie in his little beanbag chair in front of the TV.

He giggled. "I love this one," he told her, and immediately became entranced by the cartoon characters on the screen.

"He can already pick out certain characters in Japanese just by watching that cartoon," Joceline told Rourke. "I think he may have a flair for languages."

"Do you speak any?" he asked without appearing to care.

She laughed. "I can barely speak my own language."

"Then he must get it from his father or someone else in his family," he said easily.

Joceline went pale. "You think so? I'd better check and make sure nothing was taken." Which brought back the enormity of having her apartment ransacked. She was terrified and trying not to show it, because she didn't want to upset Markie

She went quickly from room to room and found that though she'd thought nothing else had been touched, she was wrong. There were papers scattered, drawers askew, even chair cushions upended.

"What in the world could they have been

157

looking for?" she wondered uneasily.

"What sort of important papers do you keep here, besides that diary?" Rourke asked, nodding toward the diary that she was holding so tightly in one hand.

She pushed back her hair and looked around worriedly. "Nothing much. The usual bills and important papers. Birth certificates."

"Are they all here?"

She went to the folder where she kept her personal documents, in a cheap cardboard filing cabinet, and pulled out the file folder. There was nothing that would prove anything. She'd been very careful about that.

She opened the folder and looked inside, and sighed with helpless relief. "Everything's right here," she said, and laughed unsteadily.

Rourke's eyes were narrow and thoughtful. He wasn't going to tell her that there were ways to collect documents without physically removing them. Any good agent carried a tiny camera, often disguised as a cigarette lighter or pen. A lock on a diary was so simple to open that a beginner could do it with ease, and without leaving any telltale mark of tampering. She was unusually worried about that diary and some of her important papers. Why?

She saw his mind working and her face tautened. "Don't pry."

"Was I prying?" he exclaimed, and grinned.

"You were thinking about it," she accused.

"Pretty and smart and reads minds, too," he teased.

She flushed. "Let's leave it at 'smart.' "

"And doesn't like flattery. I'm taking notes," he added. He smiled at her. "How would you feel about living in Africa?"

"I am not leaving the country with you," she said firmly.

"I have a nice little place there in Kenya, with a pet lion."

"A lion? You got a lion?" Markie was out of his chair in a flash, looking up at the tall blond man. "Could I pet it?"

"You could even ride him," Rourke assured him with a big smile. "He's very tame. I raised him from a cub. Poachers got his mum."

"Oh, that's very sad," Markie said. "I would feed him hamburgers, if I had a lion."

"I don't think they'd like it if you tried to keep him in your apartment," Rourke assured him.

"These two guys in England did just that." Joceline chuckled. "It was viral on the web about two years ago. Two boys bought a lion cub and kept it in their apartment, then they had to let it go to a preserve in Africa because it got so big. They went to see it, despite people warning that it was wild and would attack them. But it ran right up to them and put its paws on their shoulders and started rubbing its head against them. It even took them to see its mate." She sighed. "I cried like a baby, watching it. They had the story on the news. Afterward, I sent a little check to the foundation that took in the boys' pet."

"Wild animals aren't so very wild after all," Rourke agreed. "Pity so many people see them as a way to quick profits."

"Oh, I do agree," Joceline said.

"See how much we have in common?" he asked.

"I want to go to Africa and see his lion," Markie announced. "Can we go now?"

"Logistics aside," Joceline told him gently, "I do have a job and you have to go to school tomorrow."

"Oh." He thought about that for a minute. "Can we go Saturday, then?"

Both adults laughed.

"Children make impossible things seem so uncomplicated," Rourke remarked when Markie had gone back to his program and Joceline was serving up cups of strong black

160

coffee. He wondered if her budget would stretch to giving free coffee to visitors, and decided that he'd bring her a pound of his special South African coffee next time he came over.

"Yes. Markie's had a hard time of it," she remarked with a sigh. "He has asthma and his lungs aren't strong. We spend a lot of time in doctors' offices."

"There are allergy shots," he said helpfully.

"He takes them," she said. "And they help. But if he's stressed or exposed to viruses, he gets sick easier than most kids do."

"He's a fine little boy," he remarked, glancing at him. "You've done well."

"Thanks."

The diary was lying beside her right hand. She hadn't let it out of her sight since they'd been in the apartment. It wasn't really his business, but he was quite curious about what dark secrets she was keeping.

"What are you going to do with that?" he asked, indicating it.

"Tear it up and burn it," she said at once. "It must never be read by anyone except me. Ever."

His eyes narrowed.

"Stop speculating."

His eyebrows arched.

161

"My, you can say a lot without opening your mouth," she muttered.

"Facial expressions 101," he replied.

"Will they come back, you think?" she asked worriedly.

He shook his head. "Either they found what they were looking for, or it wasn't here."

"Found . . . ?" She was staring at him with stark horror. She looked again at the diary. It was locked. Then she remembered something she'd heard from a visitor from a covert agency, about how easy it was to pick a lock and photograph a document. Her face went pale.

"Joceline," he said gently, reading her horror, "what do you have in there that's so frightening?"

"A great source of blackmail if I were rich," she said heavily. She smoothed her hand over the diary. "But I'm not rich. And I can't imagine what use anyone else would have for it." That wasn't quite true. The right person could do a lot of damage with the information in that little book. She shuddered to think what a criminal like Monroe could do with it.

"You mustn't worry," Rourke said gently. "I'll check around and see what I can dig out. I have all sorts of sources."

She searched his expression worriedly. "I'm not afraid for myself. I don't want anyone else hurt."

"You think someone else could be?"

She swallowed. "Yes."

"What tangled webs we weave," he murmured, alluding to a poem about deception.

"Indeed." She sipped rapidly cooling coffee. "We make choices. Then we live with them."

"Do you think you made the right one?" he asked.

She smiled. "I made the only one I could." She looked toward her son, who was oblivious to everything except the Japanese manga on the television. "I've never regretted it."

"He's quite a boy."

"Thanks."

"His dad died in the service, I understand?" He didn't look at her as he said it.

"Overseas. In the military."

"Sad."

"Very." She got up. "More coffee?"

He chuckled. "No, thanks. I tend to be wired even at good times. Too much caffeine can be a real killer, in my case."

"I drink too much of it," she confessed.

He got to his feet. "I'll get working on those locks. Do you go back to the office tomorrow?"

She hesitated. "Well, I don't know," she said suddenly. "My boss won't be there, and the only cases I'm working are his . . ."

Just as she said it, the phone rang.

She got up to answer it, hesitated, with her hand outstretched as if she were about to put it into fire.

She jerked it up. "Hello?"

There was a long silence.

Her blood felt as if it froze. "Hello?" she repeated.

The line went dead.

She turned and looked at Rourke with absolute horror.

He took the receiver from her, punched in some numbers, listened and then spoke. "Yeah," he said to someone. "Do it quick. I want to know what brand of liquor he drinks in ten minutes or less. Just do it." He hung up. Joceline was amazed at how authoritative, and how businesslike, he could be when he wasn't clowning around.

"You have it tapped," she whispered.

"Yes," he replied curtly. "The minute I pulled into the driveway."

She bit her lower lip. "I'm glad you came over."

His eyebrows arched. His one eye twinkled. "You are? I can have a marriage license drawn up in less than an hour . . . !"

"Stop that," she muttered. "I'm not going to get married."

"But I have my own teeth," he protested. "And I don't even have a gray hair yet."

"That has nothing to do with it."

"A man with good teeth and no gray hair is a fine matrimonial prospect. I can also speak six impossibly difficult languages, including Afrikaans," he added.

She went to clean the coffeepot, shaking her head the whole way.

Rourke installed dead bolts and window locks. He also brought thermal curtains, heavy ones, for the windows. He didn't tell her that a sniper would have a field day with the block of apartments overlooking hers. She wouldn't have thought that anyone would be crazy enough to shoot at her or the boy.

That diary really puzzled him. He went out to get something to eat, and while he was out, he made two more telephone calls. Joceline would have had a heart attack if she'd heard the topic of discussion.

Joceline didn't sleep well. She was certainly safe enough. Rourke had kipped down on the sofa in the living room, despite her protests, fully dressed. She was uncomfortable with a man in her apartment, but she couldn't say much. That phone call with just heavy breathing had terrified her. She wasn't afraid for herself, but she was afraid for Markie. There were good reasons that she didn't advertise anything about his beginnings. Now they could serve to end his young life.

She tossed and turned. Jon would be all right, Kilraven had told her he was certain of it. But she couldn't get the picture of his white face and closed eyes and bloodstained lips out of her mind. He was such a strong, lively man that it was more disturbing to see him helpless. If he died, she didn't know what she'd do. She'd made decisions that had come back to haunt her. Perhaps she shouldn't have kept secrets. It had seemed the only possibility at the time. But, now . . .

She got up just before daylight and went into the kitchen to make breakfast, bleary-eyed and sleepy.

Rourke glanced into the kitchen. She was already fully dressed, in jeans and a T-shirt. She wouldn't wear that rig to work, of course, but she wasn't making food in her nightgown with a strange man in her apartment.

"Hungry?" she asked, smiling as he joined

her in the doorway.

"I could eat. Cereal?" he asked.

"Oh, no. I make biscuits and eggs and bacon for Markie. I want to send him to school with a good breakfast."

"Biscuits? Real biscuits?" he asked, surprised.

"Yes." She got out a wrought-iron skillet. "I make them in this," she said, running her fingers lightly over the coal-black surface. "It belonged to my great-grandmother. It's the only real heirloom I have."

"Impressive," he said, and meant it. "I haven't seen one of these since I was a kid myself."

She smiled. "It brings back a lot of memories."

"Did you know your great-grandmother?"

"Oh, no, she died before I was even born. But my grandmother talked about her all the time."

He frowned. "What about your parents?"

She swallowed. "My father died, years ago. My mother and I don't speak."

"Sorry."

"Me, too. It would have been nice if Markie had some grandparents of his own."

He pursed his lips and watched her deft hands make the dough and roll it out and cut it.

"You do that very well," he said.

She laughed. "I've had lots of practice."

"You can cook. But you won't make coffee at the office."

"It's a matter of principle," she replied. "If I start doing menial tasks, I won't ever stop. My job is demanding. I spend most of the day on the phone trying to track down information, talking to people, making contacts. There's a rhythm. If I break it to go make coffee or start serving it to visitors, I lose my concentration."

"I see."

"My boss doesn't," she said with a wicked little grin. "But over the years he's learned to accept it." She put the biscuits in the preheated oven. "He looked terrible," she said, her expression far away.

"Gunshot victims mostly do," he said. "But his injuries were slight, compared to what they could have been, I assure you."

She turned to look at him. "You think he'll really be all right?" she asked, concerned.

"Of course."

She studied him intently for a moment. "You've been shot," she said.

He nodded, and he didn't smile. "Twice. Once in the chest, once in the leg. Neither occasion was pleasant."

"They say Africa is a very dangerous place."

"It is," he agreed. "It depends on where you go. But violence is international. You find it in a lot of places."

"I guess so."

"I am South African, but I have a place in Kenya, near a game preserve," he told her, and his expression was wistful. "I have a manager there to oversee it, but I miss being able to do that myself. I spend a lot of time traveling. More than I like."

"You work in a dangerous profession."

He pursed his lips. "Dear girl, you don't know what my profession is."

"Oh, I think I could make an educated guess," she retorted.

"Which would be wrong. I don't work outside the law."

"Well!"

He nodded. "You remember that."

She laughed and shook her head.

She took Markie to school. She took time to talk to Mr. Morrison about the break-in and the threat by Monroe. He was furious that someone would threaten a child. He promised to keep a careful eye on Markie and make sure his teacher knew the situation.

Then she drove to the hospital. She knew she was going to have a war trying to get past Cammy Blackhawk, but she was going anyway. She couldn't go on with her job and her life without knowing for herself how Jon was.

She walked into the lobby and up to the desk, to ask which room in ICU he was in and if she could see him. But they'd already moved him out of ICU into a room, she was told. Her heart lifted. He couldn't be dying if they'd done that!

It turned out to be a private room on the second floor, very clean and bright. She stopped in the doorway, gripping her purse, waiting for Cammy to explode out into the hall and tell her to go away.

Jon turned his head on the pillow and spotted her. His dark eyes brightened. "Come in."

She looked around warily.

"She's not here." His voice was strained. "She's gone shopping with the fashion adviser."

She laughed then walked to the bed and looked down at him quietly. "I'm glad you're better."

"I'm better?" he asked with a grimace.

"You must be, or you'd still be occupying a cubicle in ICU," she assured him. "I called the office but they said I didn't have to go in today. I told them I was coming to see you," she added. "Everyone sends their regards and some of the other agents in your squad are coming to see you as soon as visitors are allowed."

"I work with a great group of people." He drew in a painful breath. "I'm going home to Oklahoma, to the ranch, when they release me. I won't be able to work at the office for a couple of weeks, and the scenery is better there. So is the security," he added grimly. He looked at her pointedly. "You're coming with me."

Her heart flipped over. "I . . . I . . . what?"

"You and the child," he said curtly. "Rourke told my brother what happened. You're not going to be killed because I made an enemy."

Her legs felt wobbly. "I can't go to Oklahoma," she said quickly. "I'd have to take a leave of absence and take Markie out of school . . . !"

"Details that can be worked out quite easily. I sent Mac to deal with all that." He waved an elegant hand and winced at the movement.

"But . . . !"

"Don't argue," he said heavily. "I'm in no condition for a fight."

She bit her lower lip. There were a dozen good reasons why she shouldn't let Markie be anywhere around this man, ever. She couldn't find an argument that would work without telling the truth, which would never do.

"It's a nice ranch," he said curtly. "Your son loves animals. He can even ride a horse."

"No!"

"Joceline, both Mac and I were riding ponies at the age of three," he told her. "I wouldn't let him get hurt. We have cowboys trained to work with disabled children who come to the ranch to ride our horses."

"You do?" She was surprised. She'd never thought that disabled people could ride.

"Yes." He shifted and grimaced. He was sore and sick. He hated being confined to a bed, being hospitalized. It was the first time in his law enforcement career that he'd suffered a bullet wound. He could remember vividly the sense of sudden slowing when the bullet hit. He'd not felt the pain at first, just a hard blow, like a fist in his back. Then everything slowed down and he saw the sidewalk coming up to hit him, and felt blood in his mouth. It had been an absolute shock.

"You shouldn't be moving around," Joce-

172

line said, concerned. "You might reopen the wound."

He glared at her. "I have my mother to harass me about such things. I don't need you to help her!"

She bit her lip again. Faint color touched her cheeks. "Sorry. Slip of the tongue. Won't happen again." She crossed her heart.

He laughed despite himself and then groaned, because it hurt.

"Another slip. Very sorry," she said quickly. "I just wanted to see you, to make sure that you were all right."

"I got shot," he said icily. "I'm not all right!"

"You're not dead, either," she reminded him.

He sank back on the pillows and fiddled with the lightweight sheet and blanket that covered him. The hospital gown was barely visible above it. "I'm freezing to death," he muttered. "I want a real blanket and a comforter. And I want to go home!"

The nurse stuck her head around the door and grimaced. "Sir, could you complain in a little quieter manner?" she asked gently. "There's a gentleman next door recuperating from a knife wound. He's trying to sleep."

Jon glared at her.

She cleared her throat, and walked back out.

Jon muttered unspeakable things under his breath.

"Your mother will have kittens if you even suggest taking me to Oklahoma," Joceline told him firmly. "I cannot work in a combat zone."

He sighed. "Neither can I, really, but what sort of choice do we have?" he asked. His black eyes narrowed. "Rourke told me that you had a break-in at your apartment and that there was a harassing phone call."

She looked as tired as she felt. "Yes. We had to call the police and have them investigate. Markie was scared to death until one of the investigators gave him a piece of chewing gum and enthused over his Diego toys," she added, alluding to a children's program on TV.

Jon was surprised. "Not your typical investigator."

"It was Rick Marquez," she said, laughing. "He's sort of in a class all his own. He knows Rourke, too, apparently."

"Most people in law enforcement know Rourke, or know about him," he added. He shifted and grimaced again. "I don't want you alone in your apartment until we get the case wrapped up. Peppy may have been involved in my niece's murder. If that's the case, and he's helping Monroe get even with me, he'd have no problem shooting another child," he added meaningfully. He didn't say that he was convinced that Monroe would never have been able to carry out the shooting without flubbing it.

She knew what he was referring to. It made her pale. "That being said, I would feel safer at your ranch. I understand you have at least one retired federal agent on your payroll."

"We have three," he corrected, "plus a former hit man for the mob."

She stared at him without blinking.

He laughed. "He was very young and desperate when he did his first job. He was tricked into it and he didn't fire the fatal shot. He did go to prison and he was able to redeem himself before he became a hardened criminal. He did his time and paid the price. It was twenty-five years ago. He needed a job when he got out and he'd worked with livestock at the prison where he served his time. I talked to him there several times when I was interviewing convicts on current cases."

She was still leery.

"You'll understand when you meet him. I'll have our private jet fly you and Markie up there tomorrow."

"Your mother . . ."

"She's on her way to Paris tonight, with the fashion consultant, to see the new spring lines," he said in a droll tone. "I promised to call her daily about my progress. She'll never know you were there."

"You should tell her," she said worriedly.

"If I do, you'll never arrive. She'll commandeer the plane and land you on a desert island somewhere."

She laughed. "Okay."

"It's only for a few days. When you come home, we'll have to make some sort of security arrangements to keep you and Markie safe. I've already talked to the SAC about giving you time off to help me work on cases at the ranch."

She hated her financial inability to do anything about that, but she had no choice except to accept help. She couldn't put Markie at risk.

"It will be all right," he assured her.

"Nothing ever really is," she mused. She smiled. "I'm glad you're getting better." She looked at her watch. "I have to go."

"I'll have the pilot phone you tonight," he told her. "Is Rourke staying?"

She glowered at him. "Yes. He won't leave and I'm not strong enough to pick him up and toss him out the door."

He smiled. "He's the best at what he does. Don't argue."

"Okay."

His eyes searched hers and held them. It was like a mild electric shock. "I'll see you tomorrow, Joceline." His deep voice was almost purring.

She drew in a steadying breath. Her heart was turning cartwheels. "Okay."

He smiled. "Thanks for coming to see about me."

She shifted. "It's in my job description. Take dictation, run down leads, keep a neat filing system online and come see the boss when some idiot shoots him." She glanced at him. "But I don't make coffee."

He just shook his head. But there was a light in his dark eyes that was puzzling. She thought about it all the way home.

8

The plane was a small jet. Joceline was surprised at the luxury inside. The plane had a cabin that was more luxurious than the best hotel she'd ever seen. It had everything from thick blankets to wrap around Markie to beverage service, and even meals.

"We try to make sure that our bosses have everything they need when we fly." The steward chuckled.

"It's very nice of Mr. Blackhawk to let us fly up," Joceline told him. "My car would never make it to Dallas, much less Oklahoma," she added with a laugh.

He laughed. "I know what you mean. Until I landed this job, I considered any vehicle with less than a hundred thousand miles on it as brand-new."

She leaned forward. "Mine just turned over on a hundred thousand. But it's one of those little Japanese imports and in great mechanical shape. It should go for a few more miles."

"I agree. They're great cars for people on budgets. Hey, sport," he told Markie, "you ever seen the inside of a cockpit?"

"No," Markie replied from inside the blanket.

"Want to?"

He sat up. "You mean it?"

"I do."

He pushed off the blanket. "Sure!"

"Come on, then," the steward said with a grin, and held out his hand.

"It's okay?" Markie asked his mother.

"Certainly," she assured him, smiling.

He went with the steward and Joceline sat back in her seat, worrying again. So much turmoil in her life, in such a short time. She was sick with fear and she couldn't let it show because it would upset Markie. She was afraid to be in the apartment, but even more afraid to go to the Blackhawk family ranch. She'd kept Markie separate from her work all his life, away from her boss and his family. It was awkward and difficult, this trip. But she comforted herself with the knowledge that it was only for a couple of days. Surely in that short length of time, nobody would pry.

She closed her eyes. She hadn't been sleeping well. She kept seeing Jon's pale face and bloodstained lips the night they'd taken him to the hospital. He could have died without ever knowing . . .

She bit down hard on that thought. He could never know. She'd made a hard decision and now she had to live with it. She closed her eyes and was suddenly asleep before she knew it.

"Ma'am?"

She heard the voice through a fog. She'd been riding an elephant and carrying a buffalo rifle, dressed in buckskins and a floppy hat yelling "Lay on, McDuff!" to someone in the distance.

She opened her eyes and blurted out the dream, laughing.

"Something you ate, maybe?" the steward asked with twinkling eyes.

"Must have been something awful," she agreed, sitting up straight. "An elephant of all things, and carrying a Sharps buffalo rifle, .50 caliber." She shook her head. "I guess it was that first-person account of a fight Quanah Parker was in that I've been reading."

"The one they call the fight of Adobe Walls, where Comanches led by Quanah Parker, outnumbered them something like five-to-one, got into it with a handful of buffalo hunters armed with those rifles and they fought him off?"

She grinned. "The very one. Quanah Parker was quite a guy."

The steward nodded. "His mother was white, a captive who was married to the chief of that particular Comanche tribe," he added. "The whites traded for her and took her, forcibly, back home. She tried over and over to escape and go back, but she couldn't. She just died."

She shook her head. "She loved her Comanche husband. And he never remarried. People are always trying to make other people do what they want," she said with a quiet smile. "Nothing ever changes much."

"Never does. We're about to land," the steward said. "Your son went to sleep when he came back in here," he added, nodding toward Markie, covered up in blankets and sound asleep.

"We've had a fraught couple of days," she said without elaborating. "I don't think he's slept much, and I certainly haven't."

"The ranch is a nice place for sleeping," the steward told her. "It's out in the country. No city noises, no traffic sounds. Just cattle bellowing occasionally and dogs barking."

"They have dogs?" Markie asked suddenly, sitting up to throw off the blankets.

"Oh, yes," the steward told him with a smile. "They raise champion German shepherds."

"Oh, dear," Joceline said. The animals had a bad reputation for being aggressive.

The steward laughed. "I can almost tell what you're thinking, but these babies wouldn't hurt a fly — not unless someone in the family was attacked. You'll see what I mean when we get there."

"I wish we could have a dog," Markie said with a pointed look at his mother.

"Just as soon as we buy that mansion in France, I'll buy you one," she told him with a straight face.

"We're gonna live in France?" the child exclaimed. "When?"

Joceline sighed and explained the concept of sarcasm to him.

A big Lincoln SUV met them at the small airstrip on the ranch. It was driven by a grizzled old cowboy with bright blue eyes and a big grin under his reddish-gold and gray whiskers.

"Miss Perry? I'm Sloane Callum. I'm sort of the chauffeur and odd job man around here. Mr. Blackhawk sent me to fetch you and the boy."

"Nice to meet you," she said, shaking hands and smiling.

"So you're that secretary we hear so much about!" he exclaimed as he loaded her small suitcase and Markie's duffel bag into the vehicle.

She didn't correct him. In his day, administrative assistants were referred to as secretaries. She smiled. "I hope what you heard wasn't too bad."

He made a face. "I hate making coffee, too," he told her as he watched her strap Markie in the backseat. "Damned shame, that, sticking kids as far away from their parents as possible even in a vehicle."

She stared at him with surprise.

He shrugged. "I had a little boy down in Mexico, many years ago," he said quietly. "He always rode up in the front of the truck with me, so I could ruffle his hair and point out things to him without getting a crick in my neck."

"That was before air bags," she reminded him gently. "It's too dangerous to let a child sit up front now."

"If you want my opinion, and not many people do —" he grinned "— I think the government pushes its way into our lives way too much. You can't legislate morality or safety, but they're sure trying to. We actually have cowboys around here who wear helmets to ride a damned horse!"

She muffled a giggle. He had a way of expressing things that was more amusing than disturbing. He grimaced. "Don't mind me. I'm a throwback to prehistoric times. I don't fit in anywhere." He opened the door for her. "See? Neanderthal manners, I still open doors for ladies."

She smiled at him. "I like it. You remind me of Jack Palance in that movie he won an Oscar for. I thought it was delightful, the way he protected that young woman."

His eyebrows arched and he grinned more widely.

She buckled her seat belt while he went around and got in under the steering wheel. He looked at a note pasted to the visor and glared at it, but he buckled his own seat belt. He noticed Joceline's puzzled stare and turned the visor so that she could read the note.

It read, "Put on the damned seat belt and shut up about government regulations on private industry."

She burst out laughing. "Do I want to know who wrote that?"

"Your boss," he said, and not surprisingly, as he started the SUV and drove off. "We had a big row about it when I first came to work here. I lost."

"Most people do when they get in arguments with him."

He drew in a long breath. "I'm sorry about your trouble," he told her, with a glance in the rearview mirror at Markie, who was glued to the window, looking at cattle and open country in the distance. "Sick so-and-so who'd target a child."

"Yes," she said heavily. "It's been something of a shock that we've become involved in this. Not that I'm not worried about the boss. He got shot, after all."

"If he'd been here, never would have happened," the cowboy said shortly. "I track him when he's on the ranch. He don't know it, but he's never alone. I know how federal agents get threatened. Nobody's taking out the boss on my watch."

"That makes me feel better," she said. She smiled. "I'll bet you hunt."

"Sure do. Animals, too," he added enigmatically.

She caught her breath as the hacienda-style ranch house came into view. It was enormous, most assuredly a mansion with no excuses or apologies. There were electronic gates made of black wrought iron and everything else was thick, sand-colored adobe. It was mid-November, so nothing was blooming, but Joceline saw dozens of trees lining the long driveway and dotted around the Spanish patio with its big fountain. There was a stone floor on the patio and when she looked up, she was surprised to see a man with a high-powered rifle on the balcony upstairs.

"Sharpshooter," the cowboy told her. "We have three who work shifts. Used to be just one, randomly up there, but since the boss got shot, we're more cautious."

"Not a bad idea," she agreed.

"You'll be safe here, Ms. Perry," he told her gently. "Nothing to worry about. Nothing at all," he added, jerking his eyes toward the oblivious child in the backseat. "You'll both be safe."

She smiled. "Thanks."

He parked at the door, where the semicircular driveway flanked another large, working fountain. He got out and came around to help Joceline and Markie out of the SUV.

"Look at the fountain!" Markie exclaimed, running to perch himself on the stone bench. "And it's got fish! Goldfish!"

"Chinese goldfish," the cowboy told him with a smile. "There's a big Japanese koi pond out back with enormous fish of all sorts of colors. There's even a yellow one with blue eyes."

"Can I see?" Markie exclaimed.

"Not right now," Joceline said firmly.

"First we go see the boss and get settled in our room," she added.

"Come along, young feller," the old cowboy told him with a grin as he picked up the luggage and carried it through the open wrought-iron gate.

"It's so pretty!" Markie enthused. "Look at all the trees! We don't got even one tree at our apartment!"

"Don't have," Joceline corrected automatically.

"There's a doggie!" he exclaimed, and started running toward an enormous, black-faced German shepherd dog.

"Markie, no!" Joceline almost screamed. "Don't . . . !"

"Dieter, freund!" the cowboy called in fluent German. *"Ja, Ja, freund. Das ist ein braver hund!"*

Joceline spared him a shocked glance before she rushed to Markie's side.

But the dog wasn't hostile. On the contrary, he went right up to Markie with a slow, loping gait, and sat down just in front of him, leaning forward so that the child could pet him.

"He loves kids," the cowboy told her. "Dieter is an old man, like me," he added on a chuckle. "He came over from Germany. Notice his hocks. They almost touch the ground. American-bred German shepherds' hind legs are joined higher up."

She did notice. The dog's build kept him very close to the ground. He was beautiful, with a thick shiny black coat and pale brown markings. He seemed very happy to sit and let Markie hug and pet him.

"You speak German to him," Joceline said, curious.

"Yes. All our dogs are trained to respond to it." He didn't add that there was a secret attack command in German known only to the handler and a few of the most trusted cowboys. The code was never to be used unless in the gravest of emergencies. Activated, the dogs were quite capable of attacking and bringing down a human intruder. Considering Jon's line of work, not to mention his brother's, they couldn't take chances. At least once, a would-be killer had tried to force his way in. He'd been taken off to jail, with a stop by the local hospital to stitch his wounds.

"What if an intruder also spoke German?" she wondered.

"They'd ignore him. They respond to our voices."

She shook her head. "I can't believe he's that tolerant."

He smiled. "Considering their size and

strength, it would be insane not to have them gentle around family and friends."

"I totally agree."

"Come on inside."

He led them through the house. Markie protested until the dog, Dieter, was allowed to come inside, as well. He walked right beside Markie, as if an attachment had already been formed there.

"My goodness," Joceline exclaimed, noticing the dog's actions.

"He likes you," the old cowboy told Markie with a grin.

"I like him, too. He's cool!" Markie said excitedly, petting the dog's head.

The inside of the house was open and dotted with comfortable chairs and plants and paintings. The color scheme was mostly shades of tan and brown, with some green and even a little gold in the upholstery and curtains. There was a huge stone fireplace, in which a fire was already roaring. It was cold.

"They got a fireplace!" Markie exclaimed. "Can I go sit by it?"

"Not without me," Joceline said firmly. "Come on, sport, let's get our bags unpacked before we worry people to death trying to explore, okay?"

Markie sighed. "Okay."

The old cowboy's blue eyes twinkled. He led them into a room the size of Joceline's whole apartment.

"This is the main guest suite," he told her. "There's a smaller room through the bathroom, if you want the boy to have his own, but there are two king-size beds in here."

Joceline was still gaping. "My whole apartment would fit in here," she murmured.

He laughed out loud. "So would my cabin," he told her. "But I like cozy places. You might say I've grown accustomed to them over the years," he added enigmatically.

She smiled as he put the bags down. "Thanks for bringing us here."

"Oh, I enjoyed it." He looked at Markie wistfully. "Nice to have a kid around the place again."

She frowned. "Again?"

"Kilraven's little girl spent some time here." His face went hard. "There's gossip that one of the shooters weaseled out of being charged with her death — the one that shot the boss and threatened you. He won't get in here, and he won't get away if I find out the rumor is true. I know people all over who could put a stick in his spokes. She was a precious little child —" He broke off and turned away. Just for a few seconds, the expression in his eyes had been frightening.

"The boss's room is two doors down, that way," he added when he was in the hall, pointing in the direction. "He's expecting you." He smiled. "Nice to have you here, ma'am. And you, young feller," he added to Markie. "Later, when you're settled in, I'll show you the horses if your mom don't mind."

"I don't," she assured him.

He gave her a quizzical glance. "You might, later. Don't worry about offending me, you won't," he added with a gentle smile. "You don't know me."

He tipped his hat and walked off, his spurs jingling as he went out the door. Dieter got up and followed him.

"Dieter," Markie called.

"Let him go," Joceline said. "He may be a working dog," she added.

"Oh. Okay then." He looked up at her. "We going to see Mr. Blackhawk now?"

"Yes."

She led the way down the hall and paused at the door. It was standing open.

"Joceline?"

That was Jon's deep voice. Odd, the way the word rippled along her nerves, bringing the oddest sweet sensations. She smiled self-consciously. "Yes, it's me."

She walked in, holding Markie's hand more for her own comfort than his. Jon was propped up on pillows, wearing a burgundy silk pajama top that was unbuttoned over his broad chest. His long hair was loose around his shoulders, a little tousled, as if he'd been sleeping.

He looked at Markie and smiled. "Hello."

"Hello," Markie said. He moved to the bed and leaned on it. "I'm sorry you got shot."

"Yes. Me, too."

"You got nice dogs," Markie said. "And I like your fish, too."

"Thanks."

"Dieter likes me."

"I'm not surprised," Jon said. "He's very fond of children. We got him from a family in Germany. He was our first breeding dog. He's sired several generations of wonderful pets."

"He's gorgeous," Joceline agreed. "I was surprised at how gentle he is."

Jon smiled at her and winced when he shifted position. "He's gentle until he needs to be aggressive."

"I guess you have to have good security here," she said.

"I've had a few threats over the years. At least I don't have to check the underside of my vehicles for bombs, though," he added flatly.

She shook her head. "Your brother attracts trouble."

"Yes, and it's contagious, apparently." He reached beside him and touched a button. "Megs, would you come in here, please?"

There was a soft, female voice that answered. A couple of minutes later, a small, dark woman with long black hair and brown eyes came into the room, wiping her hands on her spotless white apron. She stopped when she saw the visitors and broke into a wide smile.

"Welcome," she said in her softly accented English. "I knew you were coming, so I have prepared something very special for dinner. You like sushi, I am told."

Joceline gasped. "How did you know?" It was her secret passion and she couldn't afford to have it very often.

"I told her," Jon said with a smile. "You came out to eat with Mac and me once, a few months ago. I've never seen anyone enjoy a dish so much."

"I love it," she confessed, but didn't add that her budget wouldn't stand much of it. Sushi was frightfully expensive.

"We have a guy on the payroll who was a sushi chef before he decided he wanted to be a cowboy," Jon explained. "I sent Megs to fetch him. We have fresh seafood flown here from California, so he can slice and dice to his heart's content."

"Thank you," she said with genuine appreciation.

"My pleasure," he replied. "It's a small repayment for the inconvenience of you having to come up here to do my work."

"I didn't mind," she protested.

"Sushi is raw fish," Markie said with his blunt honesty, and made a face.

"Yes, but our chef can also make fish sticks and homemade French fries," Jon murmured with twinkling black eyes. "I hear somebody really loves those."

"Me!" Markie exclaimed. "And lots of ketchup on!"

The adults laughed.

"I am making cookies, also," Megs said. "Would your son like to come into the kitchen and help me? He can test the cookies, if you don't mind," she added dryly.

"Oh, please, can I?" Markie asked his mom, hugging her legs and looking up at her with melting blue eyes. "Please?"

"Go on," Joceline said and lifted him up to kiss his rosy cheek.

"Aww, Mom," he protested, wiggling to be put down.

"Have fun," she called as he followed a laughing Megs out the door.

"Megs?" she asked Jon when they were alone.

"A private joke," he said warmly. "She overdid the nutmeg in eggnog one Christmas and I started calling her Megs. It stuck."

She smiled. "She's very nice. Everybody here is nice, especially that cowboy you sent to the airstrip to drive us here. The one with red whiskers. Sloane Callum."

"Oh, yes. You liked him?" he asked.

"Very much. He offered to teach Markie how to ride later." She frowned. "He said an odd thing, that he wouldn't be offended if I didn't want him to, later."

He chuckled. "Some people don't like to have him around. He knows it and doesn't take offense. He and Cammy get into it once in a while. He's very opinionated. So is she, of course."

"He hunts, he said, and then he added that he hunted animals, too."

"Callum spent some time in prison for hunting men," he said abruptly.

Her eyes widened. "That was him? The hit man you told me about?" she exclaimed.

He nodded. "He was very young and his mother was dying of cancer. He fell in with a bad crowd, but they took him in after and slowly led him into doing things he should never have done. He wound up in prison. He got out, went into a rehabilitation program and ended up here. He's been with us for over ten years now."

She was impressed. "And no blemishes on his record in all that time?"

He pursed his lips. "He did try to go after Jay Copper, when it came out that he'd ordered the hit on Mac's wife that also led to the murder of Mac's daughter, Melly. He was very fond of Melly. He had a son of his own, an illegitimate one. When he went to prison, and his profession became public knowledge, his girlfriend left him."

"What happened to his son?" she wondered.

"God knows. He tried to find him, but I don't think he ever did. He was concerned that the boy probably wouldn't want to know him."

She didn't say anything. She was trying to decide how she'd feel if she'd found out that her father was a hired killer. She really didn't know.

"This house is huge," she said, for something to talk about that wasn't controversial.

"Too big," he mused. "My mother doesn't socialize much, except when she's trying to get me married. She gives parties and invites her candidate of the week."

"Sorry."

"You have no idea how hard it is to find places to hide on this ranch," he said wistfully. "She's getting familiar with all the ones I've found, so now I have to stay in San Antonio most of the time to escape her."

"She probably wants more grandchildren," she told him and averted her eyes.

"She's rather pushy," he said gently. "I'm sorry she was rude to you. She was rude to Mac's wife, too, but Winnie took her down a few pegs," he added. "She still calls her the 'little blonde chainsaw,' but she says it with affection now."

"Winnie's nice."

"Very nice." He studied her with narrowed black eyes. "You're pretty nice yourself," he said quietly. "Coming all this way, inconveniencing yourself, just to work."

"You couldn't come to the office," she pointed out.

"No, I couldn't. I'm sorry you had to take the child out of school."

"I spoke to his teacher. They understand the situation. It will be all right. He'll catch up. He's very bright."

"He'll like it here, I think. There's a lot

for a child to do. He seems to love animals."

"He does. He's always begging me for a dog. But we live in an apartment, and it's not allowed."

She thought of her apartment, and then of the break-in, and shivered.

"We talked about the attempted burglary," he said suddenly. His jaw tautened. "And the phone call that came after it. They are part of the reason I insisted on bringing you up here, where we can keep you and your son safe. I hate that you're mixed up in this."

She was surprised, and touched. "Thanks," she said softly, "but we both work for a highly visible law enforcement agency. It's unrealistic to think there would never be a risk involved in it."

"It shouldn't involve your son," he said bluntly.

"I used to be naive enough to think that no human being would ever harm a child."

"Wishful thinking."

"Yes, it is, isn't it?" she asked. She drew in a long breath. "That's what scared me about having my apartment broken into, the fact that someone might hurt Markie. He's all I have in the world."

He frowned. "You said your . . . Markie's father," he corrected, "was killed overseas."

She averted her eyes. "Yes."

"Did you care for him?"

She bit her lip. "Very much."

An odd expression touched his handsome face. "I'm sorry."

She turned away. "It was a tragedy, in many ways."

"Would you have married him, you think?"

Unseen, her hands dug into the fabric of her jeans. "He didn't have those sort of feelings for me," she managed to say.

"He had some sort, or you wouldn't have Markie," he said, and then groaned silently at the slip of the tongue.

She swallowed, hard, and turned back to him. Her face was pale. "Please. It's difficult to talk about something so personal," she said heavily. "Could we change the subject?"

He lifted an eyebrow. "I hear that the Chinese have a restaurant where robots deliver meals to the table."

A surprised laugh escaped her tight throat. "What?"

He chuckled. "I read it on a virtual news site."

"The internet has revolutionized the way we share information," she replied.

"So it has. What was your boyfriend's name?" he added suddenly.

"Mr. Blackhawk . . . !"

"Jon. We're not at the office." His gaze slid over her with a strange intensity. "What do people call you?"

"Sir?"

"What do people call you? Surely you have friends, family . . ."

"All my family is dead, except my mother, and we don't have any contact now," she blurted out. "I lost touch with my high school friends. I had a friend when I was training as a paralegal, but she married and moved to California."

"You must have a nickname," he persisted.

She bit her lip.

"Come on. Tell me."

She shifted, took a deep breath and said, "Rocky."

He blinked. "I beg your pardon?"

"Rocky."

"Would you like to explain how you came by such a, shall we say, unique nickname?"

"I sort of punched another girl at school for pouring grape juice all over my new white skirt."

His black eyes twinkled. "Rocky. I like it."

"I'd better go find Markie. When do you want to start working?"

"In the morning," he said. "You need a little time to get over the trip and settle in."

She moved toward the door. "Then I'll see you later."

He smiled. "Sure thing. Rocky."

She flushed and dived out the door.

9

Markie was already in love with Megs. He followed her around, rambling on about her wonderful cookies and how big the house was, and how many animals the Blackhawk family seemed to have. There was a big white Persian cat curled up near the fireplace. It let Markie pick it up and hold it in his lap. There was another cat, a tortoiseshell one, that kept its distance.

Joceline was delighted at the friendliness of the people who worked for Jon. She didn't expect it. Her idea of wealthy people was undergoing a reversion of late. Not that she thought Cammy Blackhawk would be friendly if she knew Jon's "secretary" was living here, even temporarily.

"Markie loves the kitchen," Joceline told Jon while she was taking dictation for emails that would be sent to various agencies about current cases.

He chuckled. He was still in some pain,

and he slept a lot, but he was improving daily. "She despairs over my eating habits. I don't like heavy meals, but she loves to cook."

She studied him over her laptop. "You're still pale."

He shrugged, and then winced, because it hurt. "You get shot and you'll understand why."

"I'm glad you're going to be okay." She smiled at him, and her eyes lit up. "I'd hate having to break in a new boss."

He smiled back. His eyes narrowed on her face. She was pretty when she smiled. He liked the color of her hair, and the thickness of it. He liked her long neck and the pert, firm little breasts that stretched the front of her pale blue sweater. He frowned. In a flash of memory, he pictured something he shouldn't even have seen.

"You have a mole," he said unexpectedly. "On your rib cage . . ."

She gasped and went red.

He cleared his throat and shook his head. "Good God, I must be out of my mind. How would I know such a thing?"

She fumbled with the keyboard and almost dropped the small notebook computer.

"Sorry," he added. "I'm really sorry. I don't know why I said that."

"It's okay, no problem," she stammered. She forced a laugh. "Probably an aftereffect of the anesthesia, it makes you do and say all sorts of weird things."

"Yes. They said it might." But he wasn't smiling now. And as he looked at her, he felt a pang of conscience. He didn't understand why . . .

Joceline always read Markie a bedtime story. Usually it was Dr. Seuss. His favorite was "Green Eggs and Ham."

She laughed as he made a face.

"I wouldn't eat green eggs," he muttered.

"Just between us, I wouldn't, either," she whispered.

He grinned at her. "I like it here," he told her. "Megs makes good cookies."

"Yes, she does. Megs makes everything good."

"I wish we could stay here." He sighed. "They got horses. I want to ride a horse."

"We're going to talk about that. But not tonight, young man," she added. "Now let's finish the book. You have to go to sleep so you can get up early in the morning and help Megs set the table for breakfast!"

"She's going to make biscuits."

"I heard."

"I like it when you make biscuits. You

don't cook much except for breakfast."

"I don't have time, baby," she said gently. It was hard to describe her hectic job to a child. She was usually so tired when she got home in the evenings that she just thawed out food she'd frozen earlier. She had a cooking day on the weekend, when she made large amounts of a dish, separated it into portions and froze it. Then she could serve the entrée with vegetables and fruit during the week. It ensured that Markie had balanced meals, and that she did, too.

"I like your biscuits."

"Thanks." She bent and kissed him.

"I'm sorry your boss got shot," he said. "I like him a lot."

"So do I. Now let's finish reading," she said firmly.

She tucked Markie in, kissed him goodnight and turned out the light. She left the door cracked so she could hear him. Sometimes he had night terrors. She didn't like having him out of her sight, even if others thought her overprotective. He did have health problems.

She went back into her own bedroom and sat down heavily in a chair. She'd been kept so busy that she hadn't had time to worry about the break-in at her apartment, but in the darkness she couldn't forget it. She'd burned the diary, as she'd threatened to. It served no purpose other than to remind her of an episode that was both painful and poignant. It contained information that could be devastating not only to herself but to innocent people if it were ever revealed. Far better to have it destroyed than risk that.

But Jon's outburst today had shocked and frightened her. She'd read enough on psychotropic drugs to know that flashbacks could occur, but she was less informed on memory. He shouldn't have remembered anything. And perhaps he didn't, consciously, but the intimacy of being here, in his home, in his bedroom with her had triggered some wisp of memory. It disturbed her. She should never have overreacted, either. But it had been impossible not to.

She locked her arms over her breasts and closed her eyes with a long sigh. She'd promised herself that she would never reveal the truth, not even under torture. But what if he remembered other things? What if it wasn't a fluke and he was regaining lost time?

She sat up, leaning over. Surely life couldn't be so cruel. After all she'd been through, it couldn't end like this.

She got up and paced. What would she do if he remembered? It would be a nightmare.

And what about his family . . . how would they . . . ?

"Stop it," she told herself in a husky whisper. "Stop it! You're making mountains of molehills."

The sound of her own voice startled her. She laughed self-consciously, got into her pajamas and climbed into bed. Surprisingly, she slept.

"You should eat more than that for breakfast," Jon scolded as she finished the last delicious piece of a homemade croissant just before she sat down in the chair beside his bed and rested her coffee cup on the table, on a doily.

"I usually cook breakfast for Markie, but I never eat much," she said apologetically. "I don't have time."

"Megs says the boy eats like a horse." He chuckled.

She smiled. "He's always starving, to hear him tell it."

"He drew a sketch of Megs. She showed it to me. You should have him taught," he added gently. "He has great natural talent."

"I think so, too," she said. "I've considered it."

His eyes narrowed. "I can take care of the tuition."

She fumbled with her notebook and almost dropped it. "I can manage," she said abruptly.

"Why are you so nervous with me?" he asked suddenly. "You're not like this at work."

She swallowed. "I'm not used to being around you away from work."

"No, that's not it," he said somberly. "It's something else."

She felt butterflies wobbling around in her stomach. "Mr. Blackhawk . . ."

"Jon," he corrected gently.

She bit her lower lip. "I can't . . ."

His black eyes narrowed on her face. He held out a big hand. "Come here, Joceline." His voice was gentle, tender. It sent ripples of sensation over her skin.

She should have ignored it. She should have pretended not to hear him . . .

She put the notebook computer carefully on the table by her chair and went to sit beside him on the bed.

His arm slid around her. He studied her with unnerving curiosity. "We've danced around the subject for several years. You would never tell me what happened that night we went to the diplomat's daughter's party."

She bit her lip again. "You were under the

influence of a very powerful psychotropic drug," she began.

"Yes, I know all that," he said impatiently. "But what happened?"

"You . . . you got very sick and I drove you to the emergency room," she stammered.

"We came to the apartment first," he said doggedly. "I do remember that much. I remember you helping me into bed. The rest is very blurry, but there has to be a reason that I know about that mole, Joceline."

She tried to move away. His arm tightened. "You . . . got a little out of hand," she confessed with a nervous smile.

One eyebrow lifted. "Amorously out of hand?"

She cleared her throat. "Just a little . . ."

He tugged. She landed on his broad, bare chest, her hands going on each side of his head on the pillow.

"Don't! You'll open the wound!"

"Not a chance," he mused. Her eyes had flecks of green in them. He was fascinated by this view of her, very close. Her mouth was soft and pretty, with a natural bow shape. Her nose was straight, with a tiny line of freckles over it. There was a faint red tinge in her hair, which was thick and soft. He smoothed his hand over it.

"You're pretty," he said in a deep, soft tone.

"I . . . am not." She laughed.

"Pretty," he repeated. His eyes darkened. His hand speared into the hair at her nape and his fingers contracted. He pulled her face down to his. "Don't worry . . . it's just the anesthetic making me goofy a few days down the line. . . ."

His wide, firm mouth covered hers, brushing at the tightness of her lips until he teased them apart. His arms contracted gently, enveloping her. The kiss was slow, soft, insistent.

She loved the way he kissed her. She moaned softly, helplessly, and went limp against him. He turned, and a gruff sound escaped his throat as it hurt, but he kept turning until she was lying on her back. His mouth never left hers. His big hand smoothed under her sweater, over her pert breast and down, to touch the mole he knew about, the mole he was certain he'd never seen.

His thumb eased up under the band of her bra and teased around the softness of her breast, while his mouth crushed onto hers in the heated silence of the room.

"Dear . . . God," he whispered hoarsely, fumbling at the catch behind her back.

He found it and unsnapped it. His hand smoothed over her firm, soft little breast. His eyes were blazing as he looked at her, registering the helpless attraction, the utter delight in his touch. He touched the hard nipple, heard her gasp at the pleasure it kindled.

"Unbelievable," he said huskily.

He pushed up the sweater and the bra and looked at her firm, dusky-tipped breasts. "Beautiful," he whispered as his head bent.

His lips smoothed over the hard rise, his tongue caressed it. She moaned again and arched up to ease his access to her body. She loved what he was doing. She couldn't even pretend to protest.

His hand smoothed under her back, feeling the soft, bare skin, which was like warm silk to his touch. His mouth opened on her breast and suckled it, hard. She cried out.

He lifted his head to look down at her flushed, shocked face. His nostrils flared. He'd never felt anything so powerful, so erotic, in all his thirty years.

"They gossip about me at work," he said gruffly. "They speculate. You can't pretend you haven't heard the rumors."

She managed a nod.

"They're true," he said, his eyes black and glittery. "I've dated. I've even had petting sessions over the years. But I've never gone all the way with a woman."

She averted her eyes.

He turned her head back, so that he could see her face. "Cammy and my father raised us very strictly," he told her. "We were taught that sex outside the sanctity of marriage is a sin. It was such a powerful lesson that we were prisoners of our own beliefs. At first, I had so many hang-ups that I couldn't do it. Then as I got older, I was embarrassed that I'd never done it."

"We're all prisoners of our upbringing," she agreed.

He smoothed his hand over her breast, enjoying the view of it, of her instant reaction. "You're as religious as any woman I've ever known, yet you have a child out of wedlock."

"Yes," she said tautly. "I made a decision . . ."

"A wonderful decision," he corrected tenderly. "He's a great little person. You've done well with him."

"Thanks."

"The point is you've had sex." His thumb and forefinger contracted on a taut nipple, producing a helpless moan from her. "What does it feel like?" he asked in almost a whisper.

Her lips parted. "I . . . don't really know," she confessed. "It was so quick . . ."

"He was in a hurry?"

She swallowed. "We were just kissing. And then all of a sudden, it was so urgent . . ." She averted her eyes. "It just happened. It hurt a little, and then it was over."

"Damn him!"

"He was . . . drunk," she said, defending him even now. "He isn't, wasn't," she corrected quickly, "the sort of person who ever lost control."

It went without saying that she was the same sort. He didn't say it. "You think he was killed overseas?"

"Yes, I'm sure that he was," she replied, but she didn't look at him. "He was very sorry."

"Did he want you to keep the child?"

"He . . . didn't know about the child," she replied. "I couldn't tell him. It was too late."

His hand stilled on her body. He didn't like the idea that she'd had someone else. It ate at him like an acid. He bent and brushed his mouth over her taut breast, enjoying the sounds of pleasure that she emitted when he did it. He could erase the bad memory. He could pleasure her, like this, but more. Much more.

His mouth became insistent. She shivered.

The pleasure was quickly becoming unmanageable.

She felt his hand at the fastening of her slacks and she caught his wrist.

"No," she whispered urgently. "We can't!"

He was almost too far gone to stop. He fought with his own instincts, visibly, trying to backtrack.

His eyes went to the door, which was standing half open. He laughed in spite of himself.

She followed his gaze and colored even more. "Oh, dear."

He pulled her sweater down. "Do you want me to apologize?" he asked.

She searched his eyes. "You're not sorry," she replied, trying to make a joke of it.

"No, I'm not," he replied, and his black eyes twinkled. "You taste like honey."

She flushed and scrambled to her feet. She fumbled the catch of her bra back into place, pulled down her sweater and tried to smooth her hair with her hands.

"There's a brush on the dresser," he said helpfully. He was lying with his face propped on a hand, watching her with obvious pleasure.

She went to get it. She smoothed it over her hair and then noticed his. Without thinking, she went and sat down on the bed beside him and ran the brush over his long, thick hair. He sat up to give her access.

"Your hair is beautiful," she said while she brushed it. "Your brother and I saw it all tangled when you were shot. We said you'd hate having it out of place."

"I would." He watched her face, smiling. "I've never let a woman brush it."

She smiled. "I'm flattered."

When she finished, he took the brush from her and brushed her own hair. "Mutual grooming. A predictable behavior in primate society."

She laughed. "Is it?"

His fingers touched her swollen mouth. "How long have we been together?" he asked.

"A long time. Almost five years."

"And we didn't know each other at all."

She nodded silently. Reality was working its way into her mind. She'd let her boss kiss her. More than kiss her. He had a mother who ate live rattlesnakes and who hated her guts. She had a child who would complicate everything.

"Stop thinking," he told her firmly. "We'll take it one step at a time. No pressure."

She met his eyes worriedly. "Your mother hates me," she stated.

"Cammy is a puff adder."

She blinked. "Excuse me?"

"It's a snake. Friend of mine from Georgia told me about them. They're nonpoisonous, but they can raise up on their tails and spread their cheeks and hiss like a cobra. But if someone goes at them with a stick, they faint from fear."

She burst out laughing. "A defensive behavior."

"Yes. Cammy's like that. She's all marshmallow inside. But she's learned to hide it from people by being obnoxious."

Joceline didn't think that was the case. But it was so new, and wonderful, to have Jon looking at her this way that she didn't voice her opinion.

She stood up. "We should get back to work."

He smiled. "Yes. We probably should."

She put up the brush and sat back down with the notebook computer in her lap. He stared at her warmly for a long moment before he began dictating again.

Joceline didn't know how to handle the new situation. She was afraid that Jon was going to want more from her than she could give. She had grave misgivings about her place in his life, and a real fear of his mother's reaction if they became involved. Then, too, there was Markie. How he was

216

going to fit into this scenario was the most frightening part of it.

And into this worry came, quite suddenly, two new complications. There was a call. It came into the main phone line at the ranch, and picked up by the message machine. The caller was brief, and blunt, and threatening.

"You're all dead, now," he said. "The kid goes first. You don't hurt my family and live to tell about it."

Jon heard it before the others did. He had a trace put on the call, but it came from a cell tower miles away, and they couldn't get beyond that. He called the local FBI office. They sent out a couple of men with electronic equipment to set up a network.

Then Joceline made some phone calls and discovered to her utter shock that Harold Monroe had been formally charged with the murder of McKuen Kilraven's little girl, Melly. There was a witness who had come forward to offer testimony, a man who had been in the cell with Monroe and who had heard him brag about his part in the killing during his weeks in jail waiting for trial on the human trafficking charge that was dropped. Monroe had been stupid enough to tell the man about the murder weapon and his ingenuity in hiding it in a public place. The police, led by Rick Marquez, on a tip from Jon, who'd spoken to a contact, had subsequently searched the culvert right outside the San Antonio Police Department and found the shotgun — the murder weapon — tucked in a garbage bag with Monroe's fingerprints on the stock of the gun, they said. A stupid mistake. A very stupid mistake, by a stupid man who thought the police were too dumb to ever catch and convict him.

Jon was in shock, as well. None of them had ever thought that Harold Monroe, the idiot nephew-by-marriage of Jay Copper, was even smart enough to use a shotgun, much less kill a child with it. All the evidence had pointed to Copper's nephew Peppy Hancock. It was the most convoluted set of circumstances Jon had ever seen in his years of law enforcement, and it went against the odds in every way. It was almost as if the charge had been contrived, for some inexplicable purpose.

Jon was worried about what his brother might do. Mac had loved his child very much. They were certain that a dead man, Dan Jones, had been involved in her murder, and Jay Copper had been arrested and prosecuted for engineering it. Mac had even heard Copper say that Peppy had been sent to assure that the hit went down. But now it seemed there was another shooter, in fact, the main shooter, whom no one had suspected and who was just being charged. Monroe blamed Jon and even his "secretary" and her child for his getting caught.

Jay Copper had dangerous contacts. The voice on the phone, which had to have been Monroe's, had promised retribution and Jon couldn't afford to underestimate the caller's intent.

So he called his brother, reluctantly, and asked him to get Rourke to come to the ranch and provide extra backup.

"I thought you liked him," Joceline said curiously when he told her about it.

"I do." But he didn't look as if he did. He was remembering his mother's comment that Rourke was unmarried and apparently interested in Joceline. He didn't want the competition, especially right now, in the beginning stages of a new, breathlessly romantic relationship between them.

"Do you like him?" Jon asked her with faint antagonism.

"Well, yes, but only as a friend," she said at once.

He seemed less rigid after that.

But Joceline was remembering something that the trip had knocked out of her mind. Someone had broken into her apartment.

She'd burned the diary, but what if someone had photographed it?

She was still brooding about the break-in when Kilraven showed up at the ranch without Winnie, and in a cold and threatening mood.

"They've got Harold Monroe in jail again," Jon said at once. "But this time he won't slip through the cracks, with or without some hotshot attorney paid for by his wife's uncle Jay."

"You think so?" Kilraven asked in an icy tone. "He just made bail."

Jon sat straight up in bed, wincing from the movement. "He what?"

"He has contacts," Kilraven said icily. "Those contacts have contacts. They found a judge who released him on a half-million-dollar bond. His attorney assured the judge that he was no flight risk."

"Which judge?" Jon wanted to know.

Kilraven named a young judge just elected to the bench the previous year.

"Him," Jon said irritably. "He'd sign off on a serial killer's bond, on humanitarian grounds."

Kilraven's eyebrows arched. It was unusual, to say the least, to have his somber and politically correct younger brother sound off about a judge or anyone connected to the judicial system.

"He's naive for someone that intelligent."

Jon's black eyes glittered. "Somebody, probably Harold Monroe, called here and made threats," he told his brother. "Most significantly, he's threatening Joceline's son."

Kilraven studied him quietly. "Like the boy, don't you?"

"Yes," Jon said at once. He smiled. "He's intelligent and quite talented with an art pencil. I told Joceline he should have lessons."

"Melly liked to draw," Kilraven replied, his eyes somber as he recalled his daughter's last drawing before her tragic death.

"She had talent," Jon agreed. "I'm sorry," he added gently. "I know it must sting to have another hand in Melly's murder revealed. But he won't get away with it, in spite of the judge's little faux pas."

"I'm not so sure. Jay Copper has property down in the Caribbean. Monroe could fly down there and hide out forever."

Kilraven just smiled.

"What do you know that I don't?" Jon demanded.

"Monroe has his own personal shadow," he said complacently. "And no, I will not tell you who it is."

"Rourke," Jon said at once, glowering.

Kilraven's eyebrows arched. "I've got Rourke watching Joceline and her son."

"He's here?" Jon exclaimed, and sat up straighter, wincing again, as he looked around as if he expected to find the man in his room.

"He's been here since they arrived," Kilraven informed him. "He keeps a low profile, so that nobody knows he's around until they need to know."

"If my employees missed him, several of them will be looking for new jobs," he said flatly.

Kilraven chuckled. "That old-timer of yours spotted him immediately and stuck a .45 revolver in his back. Rourke said he almost had to change pants, it was such a shock."

Jon smiled in spite of himself. "You know who that old-timer is."

"Of course I do." He grinned.

"I feel better, knowing that. I don't like people walking around here under the radar."

"It has to be that way," Kilraven said gently. "We can't put Joceline's child at risk."

"No. We certainly can't."

"I need to talk to her. About the break-in

at her apartment."

Jon frowned. "Do they have a suspect?"

"Not unless you mean Harold Monroe," he said, "or one of his cronies. No, it's about something in the apartment that they might have been looking for. Rick Marquez can't get an expense voucher to fly up here and question her, so I'm standing in for him." The way he said it was just a little too casual.

"Really?" Jon murmured, unconvinced.

"Really." Kilraven had a straight face. "Why are you so suspicious?"

"It's not like you to do favors for the police."

He shrugged. "Rick isn't your typical detective."

Jon thought about that, and then relaxed. "No," he replied after a minute. "He's not. She'll be in the kitchen, I imagine. She sees to Markie's meal before she has hers."

"I'll just pop in and have a word with her," Kilraven said.

"You sound like him."

"Him?"

"Rourke," he said, and made the man's name sound like a snarl.

Kilraven had to fight back a grin. It was quite obvious to him that his brother was jealous of Rourke, and not because of the sort of work he did.

"I'll work on my accent," he replied. "You doing better?" he added with genuine concern.

"Yes. It's just slower than I'd like. I want to get back to my office and make sure Harold Monroe doesn't leave the country before his trial."

"I'm going to make sure of that," Kilraven said quietly. "If he had a hand in Melly's death, and I think he did, he'll never escape justice."

"Just make sure you aren't dishing it out," Jon replied firmly. "I don't want to lose the only brother I've got. And you have a child on the way. Any day."

"I know that." Kilraven sighed heavily. "It's just hard, dealing with this. I thought it was all wrapped up when we knew Dan Jones had done the killings on orders from Jay Copper. I never dreamed there was another shooter. Then we were so sure it was Peppy Hancock, but he had an airtight alibi from a young woman for the night in question. How the hell did Monroe pull off something so involved without blabbing before this? He can't keep his mouth shut."

"I don't know. It's odd, isn't it?"

"Jay Copper said he sent Peppy to help make sure Dan Jones did what he was told.

We couldn't prove it because without the missing tape it was just hearsay evidence, so Peppy couldn't be formally charged for involvement. And now it's Hancock's idiot brother-in-law Harold Monroe, of all people, who's been arrested for the murder of my wife and child."

"After weaseling out of a human trafficking charge." He frowned. "Why did he target Joceline and the boy? Was it because she works for me?"

"Why else?" Kilraven asked with a bland expression.

Jon laid back down with a long sigh. "I hate having her in danger, having the boy under a threat."

"We'll take care of both of them," Kilraven assured him. "You just concentrate on getting well. Okay?"

Jon smiled. "Okay."

Kilraven shrugged. "I'm glad you're going to be all right."

Jon's eyes twinkled. "Thanks."

Kilraven chuckled. "You're the only brother I've got, even if your hang-ups are an ongoing embarrassment to me."

"Look who's talking!"

"And on that note, I'm leaving," Kilraven

said with a grin. "I'll see you again before I leave."

"I'll count on that."

10

Kilraven found Joceline in the kitchen, just mopping up Markie's face. He was laughing as she tickled his nose with the napkin.

They both looked up when he entered the room.

"Well, that must have been a good lunch," he told the boy with a smile.

"It was great!" Markie said.

"Megs is putting that new cartoon movie on for you to watch in the living room," he told the child. "I hear you really want to see it."

"Oh, I do! Thanks!"

"Our pleasure."

Megs came to the door and motioned to the boy, smiling at the adults as she did so.

"See you later, Mom," Markie called as he ran toward Megs.

"He's a really fine youngster," Kilraven said quietly.

"Thanks. I think so."

He turned back to her, and he wasn't smiling. "Ever hear of the Locard Exchange Principle?"

She searched his eyes. "Of course. Every criminal who steals something leaves some trace of his presence behind."

"Rourke has few peers in evidence gathering. He found a partial fingerprint on the table by your bed. It's consistent with prints on file."

She bit her lower lip. "Whose prints?"

"A former cat burglar who did odd jobs for Jay Copper."

Her face grew taut. "Why was he in my apartment? I don't have anything worth stealing."

"You kept a diary, Rourke said," he replied.

She bit her lower lip, hard. "I burned it."

"Any decent burglar can make a photographic copy of a document without taking the original."

She swallowed her fear. "That would indicate a blackmail attempt. But I don't know anything that could hurt anyone else."

"Come in here a minute, will you?"

He opened the door to the library. She hesitated, but he looked so somber that she went inside and let him close the door behind them.

"You went to a party with Jon a little over four years ago," he said without preamble. "He was given a psychotropic drug, without his knowledge, and he wound up in the hospital. You drove him there."

"Yes. It was a sick joke by the boyfriend of the girl he rescued from a kidnapping," she said.

"Soon after that, you tried to quit your job. And very soon after that, you became pregnant."

She averted her eyes. "I went out with a friend and we had too much to drink . . ." she began.

"My brother is the father of your child. Here, look out . . . !"

He caught her as she started to fall. He put her on the sofa and pushed her head down, gently, until the wave of nausea passed.

"Damn," he exclaimed softly. "I'm sorry. I should have been more careful."

She swallowed, and then swallowed again. Tears welled up in her eyes. "You're just guessing," she bit off.

"I'm not," he replied quietly. He sat down beside her. "Your son's blood type is A positive. So is Jon's. I checked dates. According to the police report, you went to the party with Jon almost exactly nine months before

229

Markie was born."

"Dates can be coincidental. And a lot of people share the same blood type," she began helplessly.

"I don't know what was in that diary, but I can guess," he continued. "You have to tell Jon, before he finds it out from Harold Monroe or someone in his organization."

She looked up with tortured eyes. "And you think he'd believe me?" she asked, incredulously. "Why do you think I kept it to myself all this time?"

"You were the only woman he ever took to a party," he said.

"Yes, and he's rich and I could barely pay my rent," she said coldly. "He didn't even know me that well. He'd have thought that I was blaming him to make a nice little secure nest egg for myself."

"That's cynical."

"Sure it is," she replied. "But it would have been his first thought. It would probably still be your mother's. We all know how she feels about her son."

He searched her tormented eyes. "Would you rather he heard it on the six o'clock news? That's the sort of thing Monroe would consider good fun."

She sat up straight. "You're assuming that Harold Monroe is the one who sent the burglar to my apartment. You're also assuming that he photographed my diary."

"They're good assumptions. Why else would he have been there?"

She frowned. "How would he even have known about the diary?"

He was frowning now, also. "Then why go into your apartment?"

"Exactly. He was looking for something he thought I had." Her eyes narrowed in concentration, then suddenly she sat up abruptly "Wait a minute . . . I'd forgotten something . . . There was a file detailing personal and criminal information about Bart Hancock. I was going to transcribe it, but the day Jon was shot I took the file home to work on it. It was the day of the robbery at my apartment . . . !"

"Did you take it back?"

"I couldn't find it," she said, flushing. "I was going to tell the boss, but then after Jon got shot and the robbery at my place, I was so upset that I forgot all about it. Oh, boy, am I in trouble! They'll fire me for incompetence . . . !"

"They won't. But the D.A. needs to know about that file. I'll talk to him."

She was almost prostrate with relief. Until she realized that she'd spilled the beans to Kilraven. She looked at him with horror.

"I'm not going to tell Jon about Markie," he assured her gently. "But you have to. You know that."

"I'm not telling him," she said stubbornly. "And you're not telling him. He'd never believe it. He'd only think I was lying out of greed. I've told people for years that Markie's father was in the military and he died overseas. I'm not changing that story now."

He looked at the stubborn set of her features. "How do you think Jon is going to feel if he knows that he has a child he was never told about?"

"He's never going to know," she said flatly. "If he wanted to be married by now, he would be. And it wouldn't be to a low-class nobody like me. My parents were farm people. My father was the first person in his entire family to ever get a college degree. My mother never even graduated from high school. She works as a waitress and her husband works as a night watchman. We're the sort of people your mother would never voluntarily invite into her home!"

"Cammy's not like that," he said softly. "You don't really know her."

"I know that she wants the best for her son," she said, avoiding his eyes. "Just as I'd want the best for my own. It's not a bad thing to leave some secrets unsolved, Kilraven."

"You're not going to bend an inch, are you?"

She shook her head. "I had to decide whether or not to keep my child," she said softly. "I made the only decision I could, but I also had to consider what would happen to Jon if he was presented with the consequences of an accident he doesn't even remember happening." She looked up at him. "I couldn't make him responsible for something he did in a drugged state of mind, something he'll never really remember. I could have stopped. I didn't. It's my fault. I was only a little tipsy. He wasn't."

"And you love him."

She swallowed again. "Yes." She looked up. "You won't tell him?"

He shook his head. "No. But I think you're wrong. About telling him the truth, and about his reaction. He's furious that I had to bring Rourke up here."

"Rourke is here?" she asked, stunned.

"He's been here ever since you arrived. I couldn't take the chance that Monroe might make good on his threat. He's a fumblefingered idiot, but he has friends who aren't."

"You really think he was only after the file?"

He smiled. "Yes."

She relaxed a little. "I'll still be in trouble about that."

"I don't think so. But tell Jon about the file, just to be on the safe side."

She nodded.

"And think about what I've said. Just think about it?"

She grimaced. "I will. But I won't change my mind."

"Fair enough."

Rourke walked into the room with Kilraven a few minutes later.

"Joceline, my angel!" he exclaimed, opening both arms wide. "We can be married in ten minutes, if you'll just agree. I can bribe a judge . . . !"

"I work for the government," she said stiffly, and she didn't smile.

He threw up his hands. "Are they all like that?" he asked Kilraven. "So full of business and puffed up with maintaining the law?"

"Most of us are, yes," Kilraven said with pursed lips.

"Don't take her side," Rourke pleaded. "I'm dying of unrequited love, and you're not helping me a bit."

"You're supposed to be protecting her, not trying to marry her," Kilraven pointed out.

"Damned straight," Jon said from the doorway of his bedroom. He was haphazardly wrapped in a blue toweling robe, with striped pajama bottoms below and bare feet lower, and a bare broad chest visible in the opening. He was glaring at Rourke.

"You shouldn't be out of bed!" Joceline fussed.

Jon lifted an eyebrow. "I'm tired of lying down."

"You'll tear open the wound!"

He glared even more darkly at her. "Cut it out."

She glared back. "Blood is hard to get out of beige carpet," she said gruffly.

He burst out laughing and winced as it pulled the stitches.

"See there? That's why you shouldn't be out of bed! Kilraven, make him lie down," she told his brother.

"I had to have stitches the last time I tried to make him do anything," Kilraven told her patiently.

She sighed with pure exasperation. "He's going to pull something loose!"

Jon ignored them both and was now glaring at Rourke. "You're here to keep her and the boy safe, not to make a spectacle of yourself with mock marriage proposals. We clear?"

Rourke's eyebrows met over his eye and eye patch. His one pale brown eye twinkled amusedly. "Oh, yes, sir," he agreed.

Jon's black eyes narrowed. "And you're not to let the child out of your sight, ever."

Rourke chuckled softly.

"Something funny?" Jon asked belligerently.

"Well, considering that the boy shares a suite with his mother, and you want me to watch him around the clock . . ."

"You know what I mean!"

"Jon, you're tottering," Kilraven said, moving to his brother's side. "Now get back in bed and stop trying to micromanage everything and everyone around you."

"I'm not tottering!"

Kilraven caught him as he pitched forward.

"Told you so," he muttered. "Now come on. Back to bed!"

He half lifted the younger man back into his room, and into the huge bed. "Now stay there," he said firmly.

Joceline peered around the door. "Is he all right?" she asked worriedly.

Jon's dark eyes smiled into hers. "Just a little weakness," he assured her. "Nothing to worry about."

"Okay," she replied, and relaxed. "If you're sure."

"Did you check with Betty at the office about that court date for Jacob Rand's preliminary hearing, the one I'm supposed to testify at?" he asked.

"Forgot. I'll do it right now."

He watched her walk away with soft, quiet eyes.

Kilraven pursed his lips and his eyes smiled. "She's nice," he said.

Jon nodded. "I'm lucky to have her. Even if she won't make coffee."

Kilraven didn't reply to that. He was busy worrying about other complications. Ones that were going to be inevitable when the truth came out.

Joceline had Jon's work caught up in three days. She was uncertain about whether or not to remain. He was healing well, but there were things she could do at the office and needed to do, to prevent a pileup when he returned. But he was reluctant to have her leave.

They'd gotten into the habit of having a bedtime snack together after Markie went to sleep. Of course, it led inevitably to hot sessions in his bed that were growing more passionate and harder to stop as time went on. Her reaction to him was instantly, helplessly responsive. He knew it and became even more insistent.

But she was able to pull back. Barely.

"We can't," she said huskily when he became even more insistent about undressing her.

"Why can't we?" he murmured against her soft breasts. "Everyone else does it."

She pulled his head back. "Because we aren't everyone else," she insisted. "And because I already have one child out of wedlock."

He took a sobering breath. "Yes."

She sat up, rearranging her clothing and got to her feet. "I should leave."

"No!"

She turned and looked down at him. "It's only going to get worse," she said miserably. "It's just because you know me and this is a new experience. You don't even like me usually."

He was looking at her with hungry eyes. "I've always liked you."

"Oh, really?" she asked in a teasing tone. "Was that before or after you threw a law book at me?"

"I threw it at the wall," he pointed out. "And it wasn't a law book, it was a gaming magazine."

He made a face.

She grinned at him. "I really do have to get back to the office. And I . . . need some space. Just for a few days."

He cocked his head and studied her. "Then what? After the few days?"

She drew in a long breath. "Can't we talk about that later?"

His face grew tight. "You're looking for an exit sign."

"My whole life has been a series of exit signs," she murmured.

"You don't think I'm serious."

"You don't know me," she replied. "You don't know a thing about me."

He frowned. "What do I need to know?"

"More than I'm willing to tell you, at the moment. And I do need some sleep."

He grimaced. He laid back down with a sigh. "I suppose you're right. Maybe it wouldn't hurt us to slow down a little."

"I'm glad you agree."

"I'm being forced to," he pointed out. But he smiled.

She shrugged. "I want you to get well."

"Me, too." He gave her a long look. "But Rourke is going back with you. I don't like it," he confessed. "But I have to agree that he'll take care of you."

She felt insecure. "You don't think someone would really try to hurt Markie?"

"They killed my niece."

She swallowed a rush of panic. "Yes."

"They won't get Markie. I promise you they won't," he said.

She let herself relax, just a little. "Thanks."

"And we'll talk some more. Tomorrow."

She hesitated. But his smile was intoxicating. Her heart jumped. She smiled back and nodded. "Tomorrow."

Joceline jumped out of bed, aglow with the newness of her relationship with Jon and hope that there might really be a future for them. She was herding Markie toward the kitchen when she opened the door and ran into a nightmare.

Cammy Blackhawk gave her and the child a glare that would have stopped a rampaging horde.

"What are you doing in my home?" she asked coldly.

Joceline wasn't usually lost for words, but she had reason to fear this woman and her reactions. She hesitated. "Working."

"Not for me," Cammy said haughtily. "I have never invited you here! I never would!

And to bring that . . . that child here! How dare you!"

Joceline bent and lifted Markie into her arms. He was looking upset already. He stared at the dark-haired woman with wide, shocked eyes.

"Please lower your voice," Joceline said stiffly. "You're upsetting Markie!"

"As if I care," the other woman replied haughtily. "You had your fun and he's the living proof of it, proof that you have no morals whatsoever!"

Joceline bit her lower lip. "You don't know a thing about me," she said huskily.

"I know all I need to. You're here trying to turn my son's head, to make yourself attractive to him! You're chasing him because he has money and you're poor!"

"You stop yelling at my mommy, you bad old girl!" Markie said angrily.

Cammy was momentarily diverted by the child, which gave Joceline enough time to turn on her heel and go back the way she'd come.

"Where are we going, Mommy?" Markie asked.

"Home, baby, as soon as I can pack." Her heart was beating overtime. She was almost in panic mode, she, who rarely panicked. She'd never seen such hatred in another

241

human's eyes.

"Good," he muttered, and buried his face in her neck. "I don't like her. She's mean!"

"You stay away from my son!" Cammy added haughtily. "I've brought my young friend here to take care of him while he's recuperating. We don't need you!"

Well, that meant he wouldn't miss out on any exciting fashion news, but it was beyond Joceline's whirling mind to vocalize the thought.

She put Markie down and started putting things into her ragged old suitcase. Cammy stood in the doorway, waiting, her arms folded tight over her chest. It outraged her that the woman had been here, with Jon, alone in her own house while she was in Europe!

"Make sure you don't take one thing that isn't yours," Cammy snapped.

Joceline ignored her.

Markie clung to his mother's legs. "I don't like it here," he told her. "I want to leave."

"We're going in just a minute, baby," Joceline told him.

The child's voice was husky and he was breathing oddly.

Joceline went down on one knee. "Breathe. Breathe. Look at me. Just breathe, okay? Don't think about it. Just breathe. Here —"

she grabbed the rescue inhaler "— breathe in. Again. Yes. Better?"

He nodded. His chest rose and fell rapidly, but with less force. His breathing regulated, just a little, as the medicine started to work.

"What's wrong with him?" Cammy asked, reluctantly.

"Nothing at all. Get your toys, sweetheart."

Markie picked up a worn bear and a ragged cowboy doll and hugged them to his chest. He was still a little shaky. Joceline was worried sick but she didn't dare show it. She finished putting their few articles of clothing in the suitcase, stuffed Markie into his jacket and put on her own. She picked up her purse and the suitcase.

"You're welcome to check my luggage," she told Cammy.

The older woman was looking at them with eyes that saw more than they wanted to. They saw poverty and hopelessness and reluctant acquiescence to an unreasonable demand.

"We'll go now," Joceline said. She took Markie's hand and led him out the door. She stopped and turned, her chin lifting with quiet pride. "Can you please ask someone to drive us to the bus station in town? It's too far for Markie to walk."

"You don't have a car?"

"My car wouldn't make it past downtown San Antonio, Mrs. Blackhawk," Joceline said with painful pride. "Mr. Blackhawk flew us up here."

"I'll have one of the hands drive you to town."

"Thank you. We'll wait on the porch." She tugged Markie along with her.

Cammy picked up the in-house phone. "Have one of the men drive Miss Thingy to the bus station with her . . . son," she spoke into it. "She's on the porch."

"I'll drive her myself, you raging old bat," came an Afrikaans-accented tone over the phone. "And you can take your prejudices and your old-world attitudes and go straight to hell with them."

The phone on the other end was slammed down. "I never!" she exclaimed, outraged.

She stormed into Jon's bedroom. Her protégée was trying to puff up his pillows while he glared at her.

"That terrible man told me to go to hell!" she told Jon, fuming. "What sort of people do you have working here?"

"Who told you that?" he asked, furious.

"That Rourke person," she said angrily. "I only asked someone to take your secretary to town to catch a bus . . ."

"Joceline? Catch a bus?" He sat straight up in bed. "Damn it!"

"Now, Jon . . ."

He reached for the phone. "Get me Rourke. I'll wait!" He glared at Cammy. "Rourke, what's going . . . she did what?" He listened. "Yes. You go with them. Take her to the airstrip . . . I'll send the pilot down. Tell her . . . hell, never mind, I'll tell her myself."

He hung up. He got up. "I'm going back to San Antonio. Get the hell out of my bedroom!" he told the blonde and his mother.

"Jon," Cammy said gently, "I'm sorry. Please. Don't get up. You're ill . . ."

"I was getting better until you decided to destroy my life!"

Cammy bit her lip. Tears were forming in her eyes. "Jon, that woman has designs on you. I don't think you really understand . . ."

"You're the one who doesn't understand," Jon shot back. He was furious. "You're not going to manage my life for me. You're not going to tell me whom I can marry, or what I can do. You're my mother, not my owner!"

Cammy shifted her stance. "You're sick and now I've upset you. I'm very sorry. I'll apologize to what's-her-name later . . ."

"Her name is Joceline," he said in a tone

that threatened.

"Yes, of course, Joceline . . ." She straightened. "She had a child out of wedlock," she began.

"So did you," Jon shot back furiously.

Cammy's face went white as a sheet. "Wh-what?"

"Except that you chose termination over delivery, isn't that right?" Jon persisted, while the blonde stood by in total shock and without saying a word. "You were afraid that my father wouldn't want the child, since you weren't married to him at the time, and you had a termination. It wasn't until he proposed that you realized what you'd done, but it was too late then, wasn't it?"

She leaned back against the wall, shattered. "I never told anybody!"

"Dad drank," he said coldly. "When he drank, he talked. He'd have married you, he said, if you'd only told him in time. He grieved for the child. He grieved for you, for a decision you'd made that he thought would tear you apart." His eyes were cold. "But it didn't hurt you, did it, Cammy, since you can sit in judgment on a woman who had more courage than you did."

She closed her eyes and shivered.

"Uh, this is obviously a very private conversation. I think I'll just wait outside," the blonde said, tiptoeing out of the room.

"You can wait with her," Jon told his mother. "I'm leaving, as soon as I can get dressed."

Cammy opened her eyes. They were dark and troubled. "I thought it was the only thing I could do," she said in a distant tone. "I never thought about how it would be, after . . ." She looked up at him. "I never wanted you to know."

"My father wished that he didn't know," he returned. "You're so self-righteous, Cammy. You're right, everybody else is wrong. You know just what other people should do, how they should live, who they should marry," he added coldly, nodding toward the closed door. "But who are you to make those decisions?"

Cammy folded her arms over her breasts. "I want you to be happy."

"And you think living with your Vogue-obsessed candidate would make me happy?" he asked incredulously.

She swallowed. "Maybe . . . maybe I've been a little overboard."

"A little." He glared more. "Let me tell you something. If I had to marry a woman like that —" he nodded toward the door "— to get a child, I'd be a bachelor forever. Looks don't matter to me. There are qualities far more important."

She shifted again. She looked guilty. "That little boy. He doesn't breathe right."

"He has asthma," he said coldly. "He has violent attacks that land him in hospital. Especially when he's upset!"

Cammy grimaced.

"Joceline isn't going to have an easy time of it, thanks to you, and I'm going back to San Antonio with . . . with . . . !" He grimaced and almost fell.

Cammy rushed forward and caught him. She helped him back to the bed, fighting tears. "I'm sorry. I'm so sorry."

"Damn it!" he ground out as he lay back down. He was too weak to carry out the threat.

She smoothed back his clean, dark hair as she had when he was a sick little boy. "It's all right. I'll make everything all right. Don't you worry. You just get well." She bit her lip, hard. "I'm sorry!" Tears were rolling down her cheeks.

Jon didn't reply. He was so angry he couldn't even manage words.

Joceline fought tears all the way to San Antonio. She was upset, but Markie was even more upset. She knew already that his agitation meant a hospital visit. He was

building to an attack even with the medicines he used.

"I'm sorry, love," Rourke said gently. "I
mean it. Cammy can be a . . ." He grimaced
as he glanced at the child. "Well, she can be
a pill."

"Not her fault," Joceline replied with a
tight smile. "She doesn't know me."

"Her loss," he replied, and the tenderness
in his tone brought a muffled sob from her
throat.

"Now, now." He sat down beside her and
pulled her close, rocking her. "Not to worry,
the world's still going around. Right, me
boy?" he asked Markie with a grin.

Markie was worried about his mother. She
was crying. That mean old woman had
upset her. But the big man sitting with them
made him feel comforted, as if it would be
all right. He smiled back. Sure. It would be
all right. If he could just breathe . . . !

11

But it wasn't all right. Joceline went home with Markie, and they'd no sooner gotten inside the apartment when he started choking.

She called Rourke, who rushed them to the emergency room. They waited outside for news while the doctor saw Markie.

"He'll be all right," Rourke promised her.

His phone rang. He got up and answered it, moving off a little. He looked worried. He said something, hung up and went back to Joceline.

"I have to go," he said quietly. "I can't explain. I've been working on a case with some other people and they've come up with a strategy that I think, I hope, will work! I'll get one of my men to watch out for you. I promise, you won't know he's around. I don't want to leave. I have no choice."

"It's okay," she told him. "Thanks for getting us here."

He pulled a bill out of his pocket and stuffed it into her coat. "Don't fuss," he said firmly. "You'll have to get a cab home. I'll make this up to you, I promise. Call me when you know how the boy is. Okay?"

He jotted down his phone number and handed it to her on a slip of paper. "Okay," she said.

He winked at her and went out the door, obviously distracted.

Joceline bent over her lap, taking deep breaths. She'd been through so much. Now she was faced with a bigger hurdle. Jon's mother had shot her right out of his life. Cammy wanted Jon to fire her and get another "secretary." She was the most possessive, rabid mother on earth and Joceline's faint dream of a future with Jon had been nipped in the bud.

It was probably for the best, she told herself. After all, she was keeping dire secrets. But what else could she have done? She'd made the only possible decision. Now she had to pay for it. And go on paying for it.

She burst into tears. It was just too much: the robbery, Jon getting shot, that horrible man threatening to kill her little boy, the possible loss of her job and now Jon's awful mother bulldozing her right out of the house. She hadn't even been allowed to say goodbye. It was just too much!

"Oh, no, you mustn't. You mustn't cry so!"

She heard the voice as if in a dream, and felt arms close around her and hug her close and rock her. "It will be all right. You'll see."

She must be dreaming, she told herself. Probably she'd been hit in the head and was in a coma. Because unless her senses were truly deceiving her, this was Cammy Black-hawk hugging her tight and assuring her that everything was going to be all right. Hallucinations, she told herself firmly. She was having hallucinations. . . .

Cammy produced a handkerchief and wiped her eyes. "I spent many nights in emergency rooms with Jon, when he was so small," she said in a conciliatory tone. "I know how frightening it is. But Jon outgrew his asthma. Your son will, too. You'll see."

Joceline bit her lip. She didn't know what to say, what to do. It was incredible, that the woman had followed her here. Why was she being kind?

"You don't trust me," Cammy said, and nodded. "Sit down. Let me tell you a story."

Joceline sat on the chair beside her, the hardest sort of chairs in the world that they seemed to love to put in hospitals.

"When I was very young, my grandfather liked to have parties with his friends. They drank and passed out. So I could sneak out of the house and nobody noticed. I liked this older man a lot. He worked for the reservation police in those days . . ." She smiled at the other woman's surprise. "Yes, I lived on the reservation in Kyle, South Dakota, because my grandfather was there. My mother had married very young and died having me. My father, well, he just disappeared and left me with my grandparents in South Dakota. When my grandmother died one winter, it was just me and Grandpa." She sighed. "To make a long story short, I was in love and I went too far. I . . . was afraid he wouldn't want the child. He was very religious, you see." She averted her eyes. "I did what I thought I should do. Then he married me and I realized . . ." She swallowed. "He never spoke of it again. He already had McKuen, and then I had Jon. So we had our two sons and we raised them to be moral and socially conscious and to never do anything they would be ashamed to announce in church."

Joceline was listening, shocked.

"I judged you," Cammy said quietly. "I had no right. I didn't have your courage. You kept your baby."

Joceline averted her eyes. "I made a decision. I never knew if it would be the right one. I knew that Markie would never know his father."

"That is a tragedy."

"A big one."

Cammy took the younger woman's cold hands in hers. "I am sorry for what I said to you. For the way I acted. I am most sorry for the difficulty it has caused for your son. But he will be all right. Jon had such attacks. They were always terrifying, but they always ended and he was fine."

"Markie has weak lungs."

"So did Jon. It was one reason I was very strict about not letting him smoke." She sighed. "Alas, I could never stop his father, and I did try. Then McKuen took up those awful cigars . . . !"

Joceline smiled. She bit her lip. "Is Jon all right?"

"Yes. He tried to come back to his apartment here. He was very angry. It was my fault." She lowered her eyes. "I worry about him so much. I don't want him to be left alone." She bit her lip and lifted her dark eyes to Joceline's. "They say I have high blood pressure. They want me to take pills for it. I don't want to. I hate medicine."

"But you must," Joceline said gently. "You

don't want to have a stroke. Dying is not the worst thing that could happen to you. You could be paralyzed. When I was little, my grandmother had one. She was paralyzed on one side and laid in her bed that way for two years before she died. It was so sad. You must take the medicine!"

Cammy drew in a long breath. "I could die anyway."

"No. You're going to be a grandmother," she said and managed a smile even through her misery. "Very soon, too."

Cammy brightened. "I'd forgotten. My second grandchild."

Joceline nodded. Her eyes were curiously sad. "Yes. Your second one."

"I suppose I should think about that and stop trying to force Jon to marry girls I like," she said, grimacing. She studied Joceline. "Rourke wants to marry you. It makes Jon furious," she added with a soft chuckle.

"Markie likes Rourke," Joceline said noncommittally. "He has lions on his farm in South Africa."

"Africa is a very dangerous place — you should not take a child there," Cammy said firmly. "And Rourke is no mother's idea of a suitable husband for her daughter!"

Incredible. Cammy was actually trying to discourage her from marrying Rourke?

Before she could say anything else, the emergency room physician found her. He smiled. "Not to worry," he said in a British accent, "the boy's going to be fine. We had to give him several treatments, but we've cleared his lungs. I think it's safe for you to take him home now."

"Will he need antibiotics?"

"No. Just the preventive inhaler. Do you have one?"

"Yes."

"And the rescue inhaler, if you need it," he added. He smiled. "He's quite a bright little boy. He was worried about you. There had been a quarrel, I gather?"

"Yes, and my fault." Cammy stepped forward. "But it's all over now."

The doctor seemed surprised. "Then I'll take you to Markie."

Joceline and, to her surprise, Cammy fell in behind him.

Markie looked horrified when he saw the older woman walk in with his mother.

Cammy went forward before Joceline could speak and lifted the child in her arms. "I am very sorry," she said softly, and she smiled. "I am a mean old woman, but I think I can get over it. Would you like an ice cream?"

Markie seemed torn between indignation

at the woman's treatment of his mother and the promise of a rare and special treat. He looked at Joceline for guidance.

She actually chuckled. "I think the offer of ice cream is going to save the day."

Cammy smiled back.

They took Markie to the hospital cafeteria and he did get ice cream, but only after a suitable meal, for which Cammy paid and accepted no argument.

She sipped black coffee and refused dessert. "I never eat sweets," she told them. "An old habit. When I was a child, we were told that sugar was the foundation of all health problems and we were only allowed candy or cake on very special occasions."

"Are you a Native American?" Markie asked curiously. "We study them in school."

Cammy nodded. "My blood is mostly Cherokee, but I have grandparents who were Lakota Sioux and a grandfather who was Comanche."

"Can you speak it?"

"I can speak a little Cherokee," she said, smiling. "We lose the native languages if they aren't spoken. I try to remember what my parents taught me."

"Jon's father was Lakota, wasn't he?" Joceline asked.

"Yes. His blood was full." She laughed.

"His mother thought I was unsuitable, because my blood was mixed."

Joceline was shocked.

"As you see, prejudice has no home," she added. "I married him anyway. They did not speak to us for two years. When Jon was born, they softened."

"Children do that."

"Indeed."

Joceline felt so worn. She was burned out, from the trauma of Jon's shooting and their changed relationship, not to mention the flight from Oklahoma with a furious Cammy at their backs. And now, here she was, Joceline's worst enemy, buying them ice cream. Jon had been right: Cammy wasn't who she seemed to be.

She spooned ice cream into her mouth and frowned. Something suddenly occurred to her, something she'd been far too upset to consider. "How did he know?"

Cammy blinked. "Excuse me?"

"Somebody broke into my apartment," she explained. "Kilraven and I think it was to get a file that I took home with me. How did the burglar know I'd taken the file home?"

"Did you tell someone?" Cammy asked.

"Just Betty, at our office, when we were having coffee." The spoon paused in midair.

"No." She dismissed that thought at once. "She's been there longer than I have. She's one of our most trusted employees."

"Someone else in the office?"

"There are so many people who work there," Joceline said uneasily. "Not only the agents and clerical staff, but we have a lot of part-timers who come in to help. We have linguists and information specialists, computer programmers, payroll . . ." She frowned. "Well, one of our part-timers was at the table, but it couldn't have been her. You see, her father is a homicide detective for the local police department." She laughed. "I suppose someone could have overheard us and mentioned it to another person, you know how that goes. It's a busy office." She sighed. "It's been a very hectic week."

"I know what you mean. I have spent the past few years certain that one of my sons would be killed by some criminal," she said heavily. "They work at such dangerous jobs, like my late husband."

"They're very good at what they do," Joceline said gently. "And very careful."

"Yes. You're right." She smiled. "I worry too much." She looked down at her coffee. "I made a decision. I hope it was the right one." She looked up. "Jon will need you, very much."

Joceline wondered at the phrasing, but Cammy quickly changed the subject.

Cammy took them home in a cab and paid for it, ignoring Joceline's protests. "It was my fault, all of it," she said gently. "This is the least I can do."

"Thank you."

Cammy studied her quietly. "You love my son."

Joceline clammed up. "He's my boss. Of course I'm . . . fond of him."

Cammy's dark eyes had narrowed. The little boy holding Joceline's hand was suddenly so familiar to her that she felt a pang of terrible conscience. He did act so much like Jon, at that age . . .

She was adding up facts. Jon's date with Joceline years ago at a party where he'd been drugged, about nine months before Markie was born; her seemingly out of character behavior to give birth to a child out of wedlock when she was such a religious person; did that add up to something that Cammy hadn't seen?

She felt a pang of conscience for the things she'd said to and about this brave young woman. She had another secret of her own that she couldn't share with anyone. She was walking into a very great danger that she hadn't confided even to her own sons. She hoped she was doing the right thing. She'd been reluctant at the time; she hadn't been too well-disposed toward this young woman and her child. Now she felt better about the decision. It was going to be painful for other people, as well. But if it would save a life . . .

She didn't let on about her suspicions. She simply smiled, and waved, with one last, lingering look at Markie, and let the cab-driver take her to a hotel room she'd reserved. She leaned her head back against the seat, thinking silently.

When she got to the hotel, she had company just briefly. She was told what to do, and when. But before she followed the instructions, she called McKuen.

"What do you know about Joceline's son?" she asked bluntly.

"Nothing I'd ever tell you, Cammy," he replied with equal bluntness.

"I went to see her. She had to take her little boy to the hospital because of me," she added with some shame. "I never felt so guilty about anything."

McKuen relaxed a little. "That was nice."

"Jon threw me out of the house," she added sadly. "He wasn't even speaking to me when I left. I sent my young friend

261

home, Charlene, you know. I remembered the little boy trying to breathe because I upset him so much. I was sorry for what I did. I wanted to try to make it up to Joceline and her child, so I called her apartment and when she wasn't there, I figured out what must have happened, so I called hospitals until I found them. That man made threats. Will she and the child be safe in her apartment?"

"Men are watching her every minute."

"Not Rourke," she said firmly. "He should not be her guardian. He lives in Africa."

"You wanted her to marry him and go there . . ."

"That was before," she said. "Markie acts and if you look closely, he resembles . . . Jon," she said hesitantly. "Except for the color of his eyes and his skin — but he would tan very well in the sun, I expect."

"You're reaching, Cammy."

"Am I? Jon went to a party with Joceline and his drink was spiked. He was very drugged. All I have to do is find out the exact date of the party and the exact date of Markie's birth," she added doggedly. "I can hire a private detective."

He drew in a breath. "You think too much like me." He didn't mention that he'd already done what she was suggesting.

"He's my grandson." She almost choked on the word. "Markie is my grandson!"

He hesitated. Then he let out a breath. "Yes. She was afraid that Jon wouldn't believe the boy was his, that he'd think she was trying to blackmail him for money. He didn't know her very well then. She did what she thought was best. She couldn't give up the baby. She loved him, and his father, too much."

Cammy closed her eyes. Tears ran out of them. "I've been horrible to her."

"We noticed."

She sniffed and opened her eyes. She straightened. "Never again. I'm going to see to it that the child has everything he needs, and Joceline, too. And Jon should marry her, at once!"

"Cammy, you're forgetting one little complication."

"What?"

"Jon doesn't know that Markie is his child."

Cammy sat down in a chair. Hard.

Kilraven noted the silence on the other end of the phone. "Joceline won't tell him. She's still afraid he won't believe it. The child has A positive blood type, so does Jon. A DNA test would be conclusive."

"We'd have to make Joceline do it. She

wouldn't. She's stubborn, like me."

Kilraven chuckled. "Yes."

Cammy drew a breath. "Well, you'll have to tell him."

"Oh, no. I'm not telling him."

"Then I will."

"You can't, either. Now don't go trying to manage things again. Look how you've already messed up."

She bit her lip. "Jon's furious at me. I deserve it, but I'm so scared. I didn't want to leave him alone at a time like this. I shouldn't have upset him." She didn't add that she had another reason for feeling very guilty about the way they'd parted. It would be devastating. She felt sick inside. She still wasn't sure she was doing the right thing.

"He'll cool off. I'll go see him, if you like."

"Would you?" she asked hopefully. "It would ease my mind. You can tell him how sorry I am, and that I took Joceline and the boy home from the hospital."

"I'll tell him. You know Jon. He just has to cool off."

She hesitated again. "I have high blood pressure. If it kills me, what will the two of you do? At least you have Winnie. Jon has nobody. Well, he has a child and a woman who loves him, but he doesn't know. What if I die?"

"You won't die. Didn't the doctor give you medicine?"

She fiddled with her lap. "Yes."

"Then take it, Cammy. You have a grandson, and another one almost ready to make an appearance."

"Yes." She brightened.

"You can't die yet."

She drew in another breath. She couldn't say anything, but maybe, just maybe, she could prepare them. "I feel it, you know. I have this awful cold sense that something terrible is going to happen. I had it before the shooting, but it didn't go away. Listen, I love you very, very much. I love your brother. You tell him. If anything happens . . ."

"Nothing's going to happen!"

She sighed. "You're sure?"

She sounded so worried. "I know these feelings of yours sometimes pay off," he replied. "But you're not on the spot with this one. You're going to live a long time."

She stared at an odd shadow on the wall. So soon? She gripped the phone, hard. "Of course I am."

"Now stop worrying and . . . Cammy? Cammy!"

There had been a sound. A gunshot. Two gunshots. Then a final, horrible one. Kilraven left the phone line open, grabbed a spare cell phone he always carried and started punching in numbers. His hands were shaking.

A homicide detective outside, Rick Marquez in fact, told Kilraven at the door of Cammy's hotel room that they'd found Cammy Blackhawk on the sofa, sitting up, stone dead, with bullet wounds in her chest and stomach. The phone was in her lap. Evidence teams were all over the room, photographers, the coroner's assistant, the coroner's investigator and homicide detectives. Outside, a reporter was trying his best to gain entrance, to no avail.

Kilraven absolutely wasn't allowed inside. Rick Marquez embraced him tightly, feeling the other man's resistance at first and then helpless shudders as the reality hit him.

"It's all right," Rick said gently. "It's all right. You'll snap back and do what you have to do."

"I'll find the man who did this. I'll hunt him to the ends of the earth," Kilraven said harshly as he drew away, a little flushed.

"We'll find him," Rick said. "I've got every law enforcement agency in town on alert and looking for the shooter."

"Harold Monroe made the threats against

my family."

"Yes, and he's out on bond, I'll give you that. But you know Monroe screws up everything he does," Rick reminded him grimly. "Odd thing about him knowing where the murder weapon was in your family's case. That was a professional hit. Very clean. Very structured. Not a hair out of place. The guy knew what he was doing. That just doesn't seem like goof-up Harold Monroe to me."

Kilraven didn't reply. He was too shocked and hurt. He swallowed. He and Cammy had their differences, but he'd always loved her. How was he going to tell Jon? And was Cammy likely to be the only casualty?

"I've got someone watching your wife," Rick said somberly. "Rourke's got a man on Joceline and her son. We're even watching you, Kilraven," he added. "Whoever did this, and I'm not convinced it's Monroe, is dealing out revenge. It could be Jay Copper. Even in jail, he can call for help. We'll check everyone who's phoned him or seen him, or Harold Monroe, since their arrests. We'll find the perp."

"Find him in time, won't you?" Kilraven asked. "First my wife and child, then my brother, now my mother . . ." He turned away. "Damn him!"

"I know how you feel," Rick said.

Kilraven turned back to him, narrow-eyed.

"Okay, I don't," Rick conceded. "I really don't. But I promise you, on my mother's soul, I will find the killer."

Kilraven softened, just a little. "Watch your own back. You've been targeted in the past, too, and so has my wife's mother."

"My best detective colleague, Gail Rogers," Rick agreed. He smiled. "You should tell your brother. There's a reporter outside. He'll have it on the wire in no time. No way should Jon see this on CNN."

Kilraven nodded.

Marquez watched him go with great misgivings. Marquez had been maneuvered into doing something he wasn't sure about, on the word of a man he really shouldn't even have trusted. But the Blackhawks trusted him. And some traps required strong bait. He hoped his health insurance would cover the damage when certain facts were known.

Kilraven flew up to Oklahoma on the jet and phoned to have Sloane Callum meet him at the airstrip, but it was one of the hands who showed up.

"Sloane's really sorry, he got drunk and locked himself in his room," the cowboy said with a grimace. "He doesn't drink, you

268

know. But he said we all slip sometimes."

"I guess." Kilraven didn't say anything more. He didn't even tell the man why he'd rushed home.

He walked into Jon's bedroom, grim and dreading the conversation. Jon looked sick and weak, and pale, and he was still smarting from Joceline's abrupt departure on his mother's orders.

"Cammy and I had a row," he told Kilraven. "Did she send you to try to make it up?"

Kilraven went and sat down on the bed next to his brother. It was going to be so much harder because of the argument. "I have some news. It's not good."

Jon studied him. "Not like you to beat around the bush," he said with a faint smile. His expression froze. "Not Joceline or the boy?"

He shook his head. "No. Not them." It was so hard. He remembered his wife and child, the way they looked. He remembered Jon, in the emergency room. This was . . .

"Cammy. Cammy?"

Kilraven closed his eyes.

Jon was speechless. He just looked at his older brother with shock and disbelief.

"She was talking to me on the phone. There were three shots."

Jon couldn't wrap his mind around it. His mother was dead. Jay Copper had been arrested for conspiracy in the murder of Mac's wife and child, and Harold Monroe had been charged with helping kill Monica and Melly Kilraven. Now Monroe had targeted Jon's family for revenge. The bastard had killed Cammy, had killed his mother, the one person they'd never expected to need protection!

"No!" he ground out.

Kilraven gathered the younger man carefully against his broad chest and wrapped him up as tight as he dared. "No!" Jon groaned in anguish, and his eyes grew wet against his brother's broad shoulder.

Two brothers, closer in grief than ever before, were silent and still for a very long time.

"We had men watching everybody," Kilraven said a few minutes later. "Everybody except Cammy. God knows why, it never occurred to me that he'd try for her. Why? She never hurt a soul!"

"She was part of my family," Jon replied coldly. "Family is a big thing to Jay Copper. He killed a young underage girl to protect his own illegitimate son, the senator, remember? Monroe may only be his nephew by marriage, but you remember Jay Copper's sister committed suicide when Bart Hancock was briefly charged with participating in the murders."

"Monroe may be out on bail, but we'll tie him to this as well as to Melly's murder. He'll do hard time, even if he doesn't get the damned needle!" Kilraven replied. "He won't get out of this with a team of lawyers. It's a done deal. He cooked himself with his own big mouth and he was taped," he added. "One of the detectives had an inmate wired with a promise of a deal with the D.A. — everybody wanted the man who put the hit on my daughter, even the inmate who volunteered to get the evidence. The inmate had a daughter of his own about the same age."

"Does Monroe have kids?" Jon asked bitterly.

"No, it's just him and his wife. He had a father who was in jail for a murder years ago, at least, that's what we heard, but we didn't check back that far."

"How is the senator's brother, Hank Sanders, tied into this?" he asked, naming a former decorated SEAL team member, who'd help them save Kilraven and the woman who was now his wife.

"He isn't. Jay Copper had two sisters. One had Bart Hancock, the other had Harold

271

Monroe's wife. The sisters are both dead. Bart Hancock's mother died when her son's involvement in the murder of your family came out."

"Sad. For her, not for her son."

"Yes."

Kilraven turned back to Jon. "We need to get you out of here, now."

"We have to plan a funeral," the younger man said grimly.

"We do, but we're having it in San Antonio. It was where Cammy lived for many years. She'd be . . . happier there, anyway, near us."

"I'd rather bury her in Jacobsville," Jon said surprisingly. "Don't ask me why. It just seems more her sort of place than an impersonal city cemetery."

Kilraven nodded. "Yes. It does."

There was a tap on the door. Sloane Callum peered around it. "Sorry to hear about Mrs. Blackhawk," he said somberly. "We had our differences but she was a good person. And sorry I was under the weather. I won't take another drink, I swear!"

"Everybody slips once in a while," Jon replied. "It's all right."

"I can put on more men to watch out for you," Callum said.

"No need. I'm going back to San Antonio

with my brother," Jon said. "We have to see to arrangements about Cammy. We're going to bury her in Jacobsville."

"You're leaving?" Callum looked worried. "You'd be safer here, boss, I'd never let nobody hurt you . . . !"

"I know that. Thanks. But I'm going to do what I have to."

Callum hesitated. "Okay, then." He seemed deep in thought. "Well, sorry again."

"Thanks."

Callum left the room.

"He watches me like a hawk," Jon said. "He's a better watchdog than the German shepherds are."

"I guess he feels he owes it to us," Kilraven replied. "Better get moving."

Jon got out of bed, a little wobbly. "Yes." The shock was starting to wear off and he felt a cold, sharp pain that was unrelated to his wound. "I yelled at her, before . . ."

"She had this feeling," Kilraven said at once. "She was talking about having high blood pressure and taking meds for it, then she said to tell you that she loved you, loved us, very much. I was just thinking how odd that was to say when I heard the shots."

Jon's teeth clenched. "Thanks. It makes it a little easier."

"I don't know how the killer knew where

to find her, unless he's watching us," Kilraven said suddenly.

"Time for a little detective work, I think," Jon replied. "We need some answers, quickly."

"I couldn't agree more. In fact, you work for one of the best agencies in the world, and I'm sure at least one agent has free time and would be willing to ferret out a few facts on the recent movements of anybody who's related to Jay Copper!"

12

Jon called Joceline with the news the minute he was settled into his San Antonio apartment. He barely got the first words out when she asked where he was and hung up.

Markie was in school, with one of Rourke's men watching him. Joceline had to argue her way out of her apartment and, in the end, accept a ride from her own unfamiliar watchdog just to get to Jon's apartment. But she made it.

She walked in when he opened the door, closed it behind her, locked it and went right into his arms.

He held her close, rocked her, buried his face in her warm throat.

"I know, you're a big tough guy," she said, her voice muffled by his shoulder. "But losing a parent hurts. There's nothing wrong with grief."

"No." His mouth burrowed into her warm throat, opened, pressed hard. "Joceline . . . !"

His hands went under her blouse, up to the fastening of her bra. She didn't protest, not even when he removed every inch of clothing from her pretty body and started kissing his way down it.

He couldn't lift her; the wound was too fresh. But he tugged her into the bedroom, closed the door, smoothed her down on the bed and stripped off his pajamas without a second thought.

She opened her arms to him, welcoming, comforting, and let him pin her to the bed with his weight.

"I shouldn't," he began.

She pulled his mouth down to hers and held it there, shifting to make way for his long legs and the sudden, sweet thrust of him inside her.

He gasped at the sensation he'd never felt. At least, he didn't think he'd felt it. But the rhythm of his body on hers was oddly familiar, like the sound of her soft gasps of pleasure as he shifted and twisted.

He lifted his head and looked down at her, saw the hard, dusky pink tips of her breasts, the shivering of her body, the wide-eyed fascination of her eyes as she looked down to where they were joined.

He lifted his hips to let her watch. He watched, too. It was the most intense sensation, like plunging into molten heat, sheathing himself in the moist darkness of her with a slow, steady rhythm.

He groaned, shocked, as pleasure shuddered through him in slow waves every time he moved.

She watched his face, fascinated. She was feeling those sensations, too. It was nothing like the quick, almost frantic pace of the first time. It was glorious. She lifted, moaning as it increased the pleasure they were sharing.

He whispered to her, shocking things, loving things, smiling at her reactions, her responses. His hand slid under her hips and moved them to his rhythm. He was aware of pain from the wound, discomfort in other areas, but the delicious pleasure dwarfed them.

He closed his eyes, shuddering, as it became suddenly urgent. He pushed down hard, deep, pinning her wrists, looking straight into her wide, helpless eyes as he buffeted her with his weight.

"It's coming," he whispered hoarsely. "It's coming . . . !"

"Jon," she cried out, arching. "Oh, Jon . . . !"

He ground down into her, clenching his teeth, driving for satisfaction, frantic for release. "I'm sorry, it's too quick . . . !"

"No . . . it's . . . not!" she bit off. She matched his rhythm with quick, sharp movements of her hips, shifting so that he was there, right there, right there . . . !

He heard her hoarse cry, followed by a moan so descriptive of what he was feeling that he moaned with her, shuddering with each penetration as the joy rose to such heights that he felt himself explode inside her.

He arched over her, his face contorted, shuddering, shuddering. He thought it would never end. He said so.

But finally, inevitably, his damp body collapsed on hers and they lay together, still intimately locked, intimately close, with their heartbeats shaking the bed.

He stretched, wincing, and lifted his head to look at her. "Joceline," he whispered. "Why does this seem familiar?"

She hesitated. Her heart was still pounding, and she was too emotionally spent to guard her expression.

"I have had sex, haven't I?" he asked gently. "I had it with you."

She swallowed, hard. She wanted to deny it, but he looked at her as if he already knew the truth. And he did. He was making mental notations, doing sums, finding answers to questions he'd never asked.

His lips parted on a rush of breath. "Markie. He's mine. He's my son!"

She bit down on her lower lip. "I didn't think you'd believe me, that anyone would believe me," she whispered tearfully. "You didn't know me. I could have been after you for your wealth, your position . . ." She closed her eyes. "I didn't know what to do."

"So you had my child, thinking I wouldn't want him or you." He bent and crushed his mouth down on hers. "You fool," he whispered. "You sweet little fool . . . oh, God!" he groaned as his movements brought the heat and urgency back. "I can't stop. I don't want to stop . . . !"

"It's all right," she whispered, lifting to the harsh, deep thrust of his body. "I don't, either." She arched up to the mouth closing on her breasts with aching delight. "I love you . . . so much!"

It was like pulling a trigger. There was no stopping then. He groaned as he drove into her, drowning in the joy of being loved and wanted. His mouth ground into hers as the rhythm grew faster and more urgent.

"Dear . . . God, it's . . . like dying . . . !" he groaned hoarsely as he shuddered again and again. "So sweet!"

"Sweet," she whispered. She moaned. Her

body shivered under the driving thrusts. She wrapped her long legs around his hips and lifted, lifted, arched, dying to end the tension, to make it like it was before, to know utter ecstasy.

She cried out, sobbing, as the tension suddenly broke for them both and they lay straining together, shuddering, as the climax shook the bed.

He moved lazily afterward, his body teasing hers in a caress that was beyond her dreams of closeness.

"This is how it should have been, how it would have been, if I hadn't been drugged," he said at her ear, his voice drowsy with satisfaction. "I would have loved you like this, slow and sweet, until you dug those short nails into my hips and bit me." He laughed softly. "I didn't know women really did things like that. I thought it was fiction. When I heard you cry, the first time, I thought I was hurting you, until I looked down into your face."

Her arms slid around his neck and she sighed with exhaustion. "I wanted you so much that night. It was really sweet, most of it. Just at the last, you were out of control and I was very naive. It hurt, and there was no time afterward to do it again. I had to get you to the hospital. Then when I knew

Markie was going to grow in my body, I had to make a decision."

He lifted his head and looked at her. "You made the right one. He's a wonderful boy." His eyes darkened. "My son."

"Yes. Your son." She smoothed back his long hair. "You don't have to marry me. . . ."

He chuckled. "It will look better if we're married. I won't be able to stay out of your bed."

She sighed as she looked into his eyes. Her own were bright with tears of joy.

He smoothed his cheek against hers. "Now we have to face unpleasant things," he said quietly. He drew away from her, fascinated by the process of intimacy, more fascinated with how they both looked afterward. He smiled.

She flushed, gazing at him. That made his smile broader. He slid into his pajamas and pulled the sheet over her. She was looking decidedly embarrassed.

He sat down beside her. "We decided to bury my mother, Cammy, in Jacobsville," he said. "But first we have to find a way to flush out the killer. He's going to pay for what he's done."

"Some of those men you're paying must have been watching Harold Monroe since he made bail," she said. "That's our starting point."

He nodded. He brushed her hair away from her cheeks. He looked very possessive. "But first we have lunch. Then we go and pick up our son from school. I have things to tell him," he added with a secretive smile.

Joceline smiled back. Even through the tragedy, she had the first hope of a happy future.

Jon and Kilraven went alone to the funeral home in Jacobsville to make the arrangements. There were two men in suits there, very official-looking, who went into one of the viewing rooms when the brothers came in.

The funeral home director seemed unsettled when they asked about making arrangements. He hesitated, smiled with a little embarrassment, showed them into his office and then left for a minute.

The door was open. The brothers noted that he went into the same room where the men in suits had gone. He was back in a minute.

"Yes, now where were we?" he asked as he sat down at his desk and pulled up a file on the computer. "Yes, the funeral. You do realize that your mother requested a closed casket and that she wanted no one, especially her sons, to view her?" he asked solemnly.

That was news to both of them. They said so.

"How do you know that?" Kilraven asked suspiciously.

The funeral home director, Mr. Adams, flushed. He looked back at the screen. "She came to see me earlier in the week," he said quickly. "She had a premonition, she said." He glanced at them. "She made the arrangements herself."

Kilraven looked at Jon. The funeral home director was oddly stiff. "Well, she had these moods," Kilraven said at last, and the director relaxed visibly. "I guess it makes sense."

"She wouldn't want people staring at her," Jon said quietly. "I'd feel like that, too. It's okay. I understand," he told the director.

"So do I," Kilraven added. "We'll need to contact her minister and we'll need pallbearers . . ."

"We'll have no end of offers from both our agencies," Jon reminded his brother. "Not a problem."

"We'll contact her minister," the director offered, "and take care of all the other arrangements. You'd like an arrangement for the casket?"

"Yes."

"I'll call the florist," the director added.

"Have you had any calls about Cammy?" Jon asked suddenly.

"In fact, we have," he replied. "Several newspapers, a television journalist and some man who never identified himself," he said, reading notes he'd made on the computer. "I thought it was very odd."

"No chance you recorded it." Jon sighed.

The man cleared his throat. "Well, we've never had any need to," he began.

"Of course not," Kilraven agreed.

The director outlined the service and they set a date for the funeral and arranged with a company to open the gravesite Cammy had already paid for in a memorial garden in, of all places, Jacobsville. The brothers had wanted to bury her there, but she'd already anticipated it and bought a plot. They smiled at her efficiency, through the sorrow.

Jon had supper with Joceline and Markie. He was sad about Cammy, and it showed. He was going back into work the next day, despite the protests from everybody.

"I'm perfectly able to work," he argued.

Joceline glowered at him. "You're just out of the hospital and your mother has been . . ."

"Yes, I know," he said, intercepting the word before it could upset him. "But life goes on. You have to come in, too." He smiled at Markie. "Not you, I'm afraid," he said with a smile. "You'll have school."

Markie sighed. "Okay, Dad," he said.

Jon actually flushed when he heard the word. "That sounds very nice," he said gently.

Markie grinned. "My daddy works for the FBI. The other kids are going to be soooo jealous!"

Jon and Joceline both laughed.

"Another thing we have to plan is a wedding, and quickly," Jon added.

"Can I be the flower boy?" Markie asked.

They burst out laughing again.

"No, but you can carry the rings. How about that?" Jon asked.

"That would be okay, I guess," he said, and dug into his spaghetti.

Jon was uneasy. He'd been so full of grief, and too fascinated with Joceline and his new status as Markie's father, to start to make sense of all that had happened. But now he was trying to put all the pieces of the puzzle together.

Jay Copper had said that he sent his

nephew Peppy to help Dan Jones murder McKuen's first wife, Monica, and their daughter, Melly. But Peppy, alias Bart Hancock, had escaped the charges, thanks to a missing tape and only hearsay evidence to carry to court. Hearsay, especially from the family of the deceased, would not convince a jury of guilt.

Subsequently, Jon had arrested Harold Monroe for human trafficking and the less-than-brilliant career criminal had managed to have the charge dismissed thanks to the retraction of the charge by the main witness. Joceline's apartment had been broken into. A file involving Bart Hancock had gone missing. Jon had been shot.

Then a witness had come forward who'd been planted in Monroe's cell during his confinement awaiting trial on the trafficking charges. The inmate was wired. He gave evidence that Monroe had bragged about helping to kill three-year-old Melly Kilraven and had even told the inmate the location of the hidden shotgun that he'd used on her. That had led to his rearrest on a murder charge. Incredibly, he was allowed bail at the hearing and soon after, Cammy Blackhawk had been murdered.

But there was something wrong here. Joceline had mentioned it. How had anyone known that she'd taken the file home? How did someone know where Cammy Black-hawk would be so that he could kill her? How had Harold Monroe, of all people, managed to pull off Jon's shooting, Cam-my's shooting and, further back in time, the murder of Kilraven's wife and child? The man could barely talk on the phone and think at the same time.

Jay Copper's sister, Bart Hancock's mother, had committed suicide when she was told that her brother and her son had been implicated in the murder of a child. Bart Hancock had been charged with the murder of children in Iraq years before, but was never brought to trial. Harold Monroe was notorious for fumbling whatever crime he attempted. He was always being rescued by his vicious uncle.

But Monroe had apparently bragged about being Melly Kilraven's killer, and even blabbed about the location of the murder weapon. Was that in character? And the inmate who just happened to be in the cell with Monroe, and offered to collect evidence, was just a little too convenient to suit Jon's sense of logic.

He leaned back in his chair and his black eyes narrowed. He was fitting puzzle pieces together. He took a sip of cold coffee, grimaced and regained his train of thought.

Joceline had taken home a file on Bart Hancock. She hadn't told anyone, except Betty at the office. And a part-time secretarial worker had overheard, but her dad was a homicide detective. Unlikely that she'd be involved in a robbery.

And Betty had no reason to want to hurt coworkers. Perhaps Joceline's phone line had been tapped. No. Rourke had put equipment on her phone for a trace; he'd have found evidence of a wiretap. That ruled out the possibility that someone had listened in on her conversation. Which took the ball right back to the office, where Betty worked.

He picked up the phone and punched in Betty's extension.

"Yes?" she answered in her sweet tone.

"Hi," he replied. "Could you come in here, please?"

"Sure thing."

A couple of minutes later, she tapped on the door, opened it and walked in. She closed it behind her and sat down in front of the desk.

"Something wrong?" she asked.

"Joceline brought a file home with her . . ."

"Oh, yes," she said, shaking her head. "She was so upset! I told her they wouldn't fire her over one mistake," she chuckled.

"And we still had an earlier version on the computer's hard drive, anyway. It was just a paper copy."

He turned his computer around. "Can you bring it up on the screen?"

"Sure."

She punched in the information, waited, waited, frowned. "That's very odd. It isn't here. I know I scanned those documents into the computer."

"What exactly was in them?" he asked.

She sat back down, still frowning, and pushed back her short, curly blond hair with a nervous hand. "I'm not absolutely sure," she said. "There was no really sensitive information in it, just some remarks by the arresting officer about Bart Hancock's mother making threats when they took him in for questioning in a local murder case. Oh, and his daughter being under suspicion for an assault that proved fatal, but that she was never charged. She was a juvenile at the time."

Jon sat up. "His daughter?"

"I believe it was his daughter. I don't remember anything else." She grimaced. "Now I'm going to be in trouble, too. I don't know how that information went missing!"

"I'll talk to the SAC," Jon said gently.

"Nobody's going to blame you. But we are going to want to know how that file was removed."

"We do background checks on all the people we hire," Betty said worriedly. "There's no way we could have anybody here with a criminal background."

"Not all people who commit crimes have criminal backgrounds."

"Yes, some people never get caught." She studied him. "I hope they catch whoever shot you," she said bluntly, "and also the person who killed your brother's wife and child, and Mrs. Blackhawk." She shook her head. "It seems they planned to wipe out your whole family. But why would they threaten Joceline and her little boy? It makes no sense. She isn't part of your family."

But she was. So was Markie. Nobody outside of the family knew. But obviously, somebody else did. He'd asked Joceline about Markie's birth certificate, but she hadn't listed a name under "Father." On the other hand, there was the record on Jon's brush with hallucinogenic drugs the night Markie had been conceived, and the record of Markie's birth nine months later. Both those events were on records that could be accessed. Someone could have connected those dates and checked them

290

out. His brother had done that, and had told him after the fact. It wasn't too far-fetched to think someone else could have done the same investigative work. Perhaps a law enforcement person with access to computer records. And they knew Jay Copper had somebody on the inside, somebody with a badge. They'd never found out who it was. Such a person would have access to databases of crimes that civilians couldn't access.

"You've connected something," Betty guessed.

"Yes. All of this ties into computer records that only someone in law enforcement could get access to. Well, legally, I mean."

She pursed her lips and frowned. "Anyone in this office with the right clearance could get to them. And the offices aren't locked during lunch hours."

"They should be. I'll bring it up with the SAC."

"Good idea."

"That part-time girl we've got working for you," he began slowly. "What do we know about her background?"

She laughed. "Phyllis? Her dad's a homicide cop at San Antonio P.D.," she said. She pulled the computer keyboard into her lap, punched in codes and brought up Phyllis

Hicks's file. She turned the screen back to Jon.

"She's working on a degree in computer programming. Her specialty is going to be cybercrime, and she wants to work here as an agent. She got the entry-level position part-time so that she could continue her college studies."

He was looking at her photograph and wondering why it seemed so familiar. "Who's her father?"

"You know him, he worked with Gail at one time," she added, naming Kilraven's mother-in-law. "His name is Dave Hicks. He's a police detective."

"I remember. Mac said Hicks was at the hospital with Marquez when Rogers got shot." He hesitated. "We never found out who shot her, either."

"Another mystery." She shook her head. "So many shootings. Marquez got blindsided, you recall, when he and Gail were working on the Senator Will Sanders case."

"Everything goes back to Sanders's arrest for murder," he mused. "Not everyone knows that he's Jay Copper's illegitimate son, and Copper is a maniac about protecting his family. All these shootings happened when the investigations began into the case that Copper was finally arrested for, the murder of a young girl who'd been to Sanders's house. But he was also charged with conspiring to murder Dan Jones, who'd been involved in silencing the witnesses, and he was charged with masterminding the murder of Mac's wife and child."

Betty nodded. "Wasn't there some talk about Jay Copper's sister, Bart Hancock's mother, being a mental patient? I know she spent some time in institutions before Copper started making big money as the senator's right-hand man."

"She did. Hancock has never been normal. But I didn't think he had children."

"If memory serves, Hancock only had one child, a daughter. He wasn't married to the child's mother, because she found out what he was doing overseas just after she had the child. Hancock's daughter would be the granddaughter of Hancock's mother, who committed suicide."

Jon was frowning. "Do we know her name?"

"I believe it was in the missing file," Betty said. "But I'll bet Joceline could dig that information up in a heartbeat," she added with a grin.

"I won't take that bet," he replied, chuckling. He picked up the phone. "Hey, Rocky, how about digging up the name of Bart Hancock's daughter for me? Yes. That's the one. You bet." His voice had dropped to a purr. "Yes. Thanks."

"Rocky?" Betty mused.

"It's an in-joke," he replied. He sighed. "And you'll hear some gossip, so I'll be the first to tell you. Joceline's little boy is my son. I didn't know until a few days ago," he added, noting Betty's shock.

"That party, where you were drugged," Betty said at once.

"Yes."

"I wondered. You see, Joceline is such an upright person," she added gently. She smiled. "Better marry her."

"The license is already applied for," he said, and smiled. The smile faded. "First, we have to get through a funeral, though."

"I'm so sorry," Betty said. "I know your mother got on your nerves, but she was a good person."

His face tautened. It was painful to discuss Cammy's death. "Yes. She was a good person."

Betty got up. "I'll file a report about the missing information," she said.

"Good idea."

She paused at the door. "Glad to have you back," she said, then smiled and left.

Joceline came into the office a minute later, looking very disconcerted.

He got up and took her by the shoulders. "What is it?"

"I found out who Bart Hancock's daughter is."

He blinked. "Excuse me?"

"You see, he didn't marry her mother. But her mother married a policeman a few years later, who adopted her daughter and gave her his name. The policeman is now a detective with San Antonio P.D. His name is Dave Hicks."

"Yes, Betty and I were just talking about him." He sat up straighter. "Phyllis Hicks is our part-time clerical worker who's in college part-time, but can't spell. And she's Bart Hancock's daughter? Does she know?"

"That's something we'll have to find out, I'm afraid."

Bart Hancock's daughter worked in their office. She had access to computer records, telephone conversations and just about any other sort of information she might care to dig out. And what she didn't know, her adoptive father could find out in a heartbeat through his police contacts. He might not even know why she was asking for the information, if she was the person who'd relayed Joceline's movements, and Cammy's, to a shooter.

Jon's breath caught. "Right under our noses!"

"We can't prove anything," she added quickly. "We don't even have a reason to charge her."

"Plus, we can't let on that we know her background," he replied. "And her adoptive dad works for San Antonio P.D., with access to all sorts of records."

"Yes."

"Well, at least now we have the beginnings of a real investigation. And some possible suspects."

She nodded. "Life just got a lot more complicated."

His hands were absently caressing her arms. "We were planning a graveside service, but Cammy's arrangements call for a public one." His eyes narrowed. "I think we might want to pay very close attention to who shows up."

"I was thinking the very same thing," she agreed.

13

The funeral home's chapel was very crowded. Almost all the employees of the San Antonio FBI field office who knew Jon showed up. Half the Jacobsville, Texas, police department was on hand and so were members of various other federal agencies who knew the very popular brothers.

"I hadn't counted on so many people," Jon told Kilraven as they sat in the front pew with Winnie and Joceline.

"Not to worry, I've got several people watching. And I've gotten court-ordered wiretaps, as well," Kilraven replied quietly. "Now that we have some solid leads, we're going to blow the case wide-open."

Joceline was looking over her shoulder. Her eyes almost popped. "I don't believe it!"

The others followed her wide-eyed stare. Harold Monroe was just walking in the door.

"Son of a . . . !" Kilraven muttered and started to get up. His expression was homicidal.

Jon pulled him back down. "Don't you dare," he said sternly. "Cammy would come back and haunt us both!"

"He killed my baby girl," Kilraven gritted.

"He's only been accused. Not convicted," Jon reminded him. "You're an officer of the law. You can't touch him. Get a grip."

Kilraven subsided, but not happily.

And then the oddest thing happened. Harold Monroe, shifty-eyed and uncomfortable, but determined, walked down the aisle to where the family was sitting and stopped in front of Kilraven.

"I didn't kill her," he said in a low tone, glancing around to make sure he wasn't overheard.

Jon scowled. "What?"

Monroe went down on one knee. He was flushed and nervous, constantly looking around the room. "I know, you think I done it all. I ain't smart. I help some poor kids get work and you think it's bad the way I do it, but listen, I ain't never killed nobody! Especially not no little kid."

The brothers were just staring at him, dumbfounded.

"And no ladies, either," he added gruffly,

glancing at the casket.

"You bragged to another jailbird that you killed my daughter," Kilraven said, barely restraining the urge to throttle the man in front of witnesses. "You even fingered the murder weapon."

Monroe lowered his voice. "Yeah. So they'd find it. I put it where I was told to. I was scared. But you tell them smart guys to look at the prints on the shells that was in it. I didn't take the shells out, you see. I left them. I figured, when I got a chance, I'd make it right. That little girl. That poor little kid . . . !"

A monster with a conscience? The spellbound audience was exchanging puzzled glances.

"He said he'd kill my wife. She's all I got. She's smart. She works in a library. She never hurt nobody!"

"He who?" Jon asked curtly.

"You look at them prints on those shells. You'll see who. And he's got a kid. She's crazy like him," he added huskily. "He took her along with him, when . . ." He swallowed. "She wasn't seen. He didn't want her stepdad to find out. She could get information from him, see. But you check them prints, then you find out where she was the night your little girl got shot. You check where she was when . . ." He glanced at the casket again, and grimaced. "Well, you'll see who. You'll see a lot."

"You confessed on tape," Kilraven said.

"Yeah, I did. I knew the guy was wired."

"How?"

Monroe shifted. "I can't say. I said enough already. I set it up so I could be accused, then maybe they wouldn't think I'd told on them. I could say, you know, that I was willing to take the rap for it, if they'd leave my wife alone." He lowered his voice. "They'll kill me in a heartbeat if they find out I told you this."

"Like hell they will." Kilraven motioned to a man in a suit in the aisle. He came forward. "This is Harold Monroe," he told the man. "If he dies, we come after you in a pickup truck at night wearing ninja gear. Get the picture?"

The man chuckled. "Yeah."

Monroe's eyes bulged. "You're protecting me? I'm out on bond on a murder charge! I even confessed!"

"We'll get the charges dropped," Jon said quietly. "You testify to what you know, we'll see what we can do for you on the other charges. If you stop trying to exploit kids."

Monroe sighed. "I ain't smart enough to make money any other way. But, hey, I guess I could move to Vegas and become a pimp." He grinned, showing a missing tooth.

Jon shook his head.

Monroe leaned forward. "You want to do some checking with San Antonio P.D.," he added in a whisper. "The guy whose fingerprints are on the shells in that shotgun, he's related to Jay Copper. But I never told you that. You found it out."

Kilraven nodded. "God, Monroe, this is going to ruin your rep in local criminal circles if it ever gets out."

"You ain't telling nobody," he said coldly. "Got that?"

Kilraven smiled.

"We'll do what we can for you," Jon said. His eyes narrowed. "Why come forward now?"

"I was gonna let the evidence on that shotgun turn the trick, but I was afraid it might fall through the cracks, especially when Mrs. Blackhawk got killed. Then I knew I had to say something. She was a great lady," he said, nodding toward the casket. "See, my dad got sent to prison for murder a long time ago. He was young and his mom had cancer, and needed medicine he couldn't pay for. When he got out, your family hired him, gave him a job, trusted him when nobody else would."

"Sloane Callum is your father?" Jon exclaimed, shocked.

"Yeah, but he never married my mom," Monroe said. "He wanted to, but she didn't believe in that stuff. Kind of a hippie, see. Anyway, I made sure nobody knew, 'cause I didn't want him to lose his job if you knew about me."

"He's a good man," Jon said quietly. He was still reeling from the inefficiency of the detectives who'd done the background check on Sloane Callum and missed this connection.

"Yes, and she was a good woman," Monroe said, nodding toward the casket again. "She made you hire him. She didn't know about me, either, but she was good to my dad." He closed his eyes. "If I'd known they were gonna do that, I'd have told my dad, and he'd have watched her."

"You made threatening phone calls," Jon began.

"Not me," Monroe replied, and with evident sincerity. "You were just doing your job when you arrested me. No call to kill a man for that. I don't hold grudges. That's why I called you, to show you I didn't hold it against you. I just wanted you to know I was out."

"Then who . . . ?"

"Check the prints on them shells," Monroe said again. "That's all I'm . . . oh, God."

He was looking toward the back of the church. A young blonde woman had walked in and was looking at him with cold eyes. He got to his feet, flushed.

"Get him out of here," Jon told the undercover agent, who herded a worried Monroe out the back door of the chapel. "Quick!"

"He told us nothing," Kilraven cautioned the others.

The blonde came up to the family, looking compassionate and sincere. "I'm so sorry about your mother," she said, and seemed really honest.

"Thanks, Phyllis," Jon said with a subdued smile. "We appreciate your coming to the service."

"A lot," Kilraven added. Winnie nodded.

"Yes," Joceline agreed, and smiled warmly.

The woman gave them a shrewd appraisal. "Wasn't that the Monroe man who was arrested for trafficking?" she wondered. "What was he saying to you?"

"Gloating," Jon said coldly.

"Kilraven was going to punch him, but Jon wouldn't let him," Joceline added curtly. "After all he's done, the nerve to show up here!"

The young woman shrugged, but she

303

couldn't hide the gleam of relief in her eyes. "Well, I just wanted to say sorry, about Mrs. Blackhawk," she added. "Such a pity. Gosh, your family has had some real tragedies, hasn't it?"

"Some real tragedies," Kilraven said quietly. "And now one more to add to it." He indicated the casket.

"It must have been devastating," she agreed. "Do they have any idea who might have done it? I mean, that Monroe man made threats, didn't he? Betty told me about the phone calls," she added quickly.

"Lots of threats," Jon said coldly. "And he's going to pay for them very soon."

She smiled. "Good. I hope he does. I'll see you all at the office, then."

"Yes," Jon replied. "Thanks for coming."

"You're very welcome." She looked at the casket with an odd curiosity, smiled at them and walked back to have a seat in the back of the chapel.

The Blackhawks looked at each other, but said nothing. Jon gripped Joceline's hand tightly in his own as the music began and a clear, sweet voice began to sing Cammy's favorite gospel song, "Amazing Grace." Despite all his best efforts to keep his emotions under control, Jon's eyes were wet as the last strong note ended on the song. But so were those of everyone else in the chapel.

The crime lab was far ahead of Jon when he spoke to Alice Mayfield Jones Fowler, their chief investigator, about the prints on the murder weapon.

"Sure, we got those prints first thing. Criminals always overlook something obvious. Monroe's prints were on the barrel, but someone else's prints were on the shells. Not too smart, to put them back in the gun after they'd been fired."

"Alice, you always put empty shells in the chamber when you store a shotgun," Jon said gently.

"Yes, I know that. I meant that he put back the same shells he'd used, with his fingerprints all over them." She whistled. "I was just checking to make sure you knew that."

"Alice . . ."

"Anyway, yes, there were prints, and they belong to Bart Hancock."

It was what Jon had thought all along. Harold Monroe was an idiot. He'd never killed anyone or even been connected with murders. Most criminals didn't step outside their comfort zones. Monroe bought and sold children, which was reprehensible, but he wasn't a killer.

"Now what?" Jon asked, thinking aloud.

"Now you get a search warrant . . ." she began.

"Alice!"

"Hey, I was just thinking aloud, honest, I know the FBI doesn't need to be led by the hand in a murder investigation —" She chuckled, then sobered. "Sorry about your mother, by the way. That was such a shock. I mean, it never occurred to any of us that she'd be a target."

"It should have. I feel guilty."

"You're human, Blackhawk," she said gently. "Don't beat yourself over the head."

"Yes. I guess so."

"If you can connect the murder weapon to Hancock, you've got a pretty good case on circumstantial evidence. Odd thing, there were other fingerprints on the shells, just a partial. But when we ran them through the database, we didn't get even one hit."

"That is odd," Jon agreed, curious. "Any ideas?"

"None. If you can make Hancock talk, he might tell you. I ruled out Dan Jones, by the way. His prints weren't on the shells."

"Even odder."

Jon was thinking, weighing clues. "I may

have something even better to cinch the case."

"What?"

"Oh, no. I'm not telling you. Next thing I know, you'll be in Hollywood pitching a murder mystery to some producer."

"Dang. Foiled again!"

"Are you working my mother's case?" he asked.

"Well, I thought I was, but they wouldn't let me into the hotel room," she said. "Marquez said they had another investigator working it."

Odd, he thought again. Marquez usually asked for Jones. Or Fowler, which was her married name. She'd married Harley Fowler, the son of a U.S. senator.

"I guess I was late on the scene." She sighed.

"I guess."

"But if you need help . . ."

"I'll call. And thanks."

"No problem."

He was now certain that Hancock was responsible for Melly's death and also for Cammy Blackhawk's. What Hancock's daughter had to do with either case was still nebulous, but Jon was going to make sure the man didn't sleaze out of the new charges.

So when he phoned Rick Marquez to request copies of the police report on his mother's death, he was shocked to run into a brick wall.

"No," Rick said at once.

"No?" Jon was taken aback.

"Not yet."

"All I want is the preliminary report . . ."

"Not yet." Rick hesitated. "I know this case is personal with you. That's why I'm not giving you anything, especially crime scene photos."

"I could get a warrant . . ."

"Yes, you could, and I'd find a judge to deny it. Maybe the same judge who let Monroe out on bail. Speaking of Monroe, we can't find him anywhere. Would you know anything about that?"

"Who, me?" Jon asked. "Why would I know?"

"He was speaking to you at the funeral home and then he vanished."

"Strange," Jon said evenly.

"Isn't it?"

Jon drew in a long breath. "I spoke to Alice Jones."

"Alice Fowler."

"Yes. She said they checked fingerprints on the shells in the murder weapon in the murder of my niece."

"That's true. We're compiling evidence right now for a warrant to arrest Bart Hancock."

"Good luck getting to him," Jon said coldly. "Isn't he at his uncle's place in the Bahamas?"

"We heard he was."

"Extradition is going to be a lengthy process, even with evidence."

There was a long pause. "Yes."

Jon felt alarm bells going off in the back of his mind. "What's going on, Marquez?" he asked suddenly.

"Why do you think something's going on?"

"Just a feeling."

"I can't tell you anything."

"Can't or won't?"

"Both." There was a pause. "What?" There was muffled conversation. "Sorry, got to go. I'll keep you posted on the investigation. And I'm sorry about your mother."

"Yes, so are we," Jon said heavily.

"I'll be in touch." He hung up.

Jon was slow putting down the phone. There was a click. With a slow smile, he reached for a button and pushed it. Things were beginning to look up.

"I absolutely can't believe Harold Monroe,

coming up to us at the funeral and denying he was responsible," Joceline told Jon that evening at her apartment, while they watched their son draw a picture of a camel he'd seen on a news program.

"I can't, either," Jon replied. "But I'm glad."

"Me, too."

"I think we may solve more than one murder, when all the evidence is collected." He shook his head. "I work for the FBI. So does my brother, intermittently. And neither of us knew that Monroe's father worked at the ranch. If we had known, with his record, I'm sure we'd have blamed him for Cammy's murder."

"I can understand why."

"I suppose even criminals have some odd sense of honor."

She brushed her hand over Markie's black hair. "You really can draw, my baby."

"Yes, you can." Jon took the pencil away from him, picked him up and placed him on his lap. "You look somewhat like me," he said in a deep, affectionate tone. "Amazing, that I never noticed before."

"You're a lot bigger than me," Markie said, and giggled when Jon tickled him.

Jon hugged the boy warmly. "I love being a father."

"Ouch, Dad, you're squeezing me!" Markie complained.

Jon chuckled and let him escape, back to the table where his pencil and paper were lying. "Of all the surprises of my life, this was the nicest," he said, sighing. He looked at Joceline, loving the sweetness of her expression, the familiarity of her. "You should have told me," he added, but in a tender tone.

"You know why I didn't." She caught his big hand in hers. "I thought it would destroy your life and hurt your career. And I knew your mother would do everything in her power to keep us away from you." She grimaced. "She really was a kind person, under that gruff attitude. I was only just getting to know her. I'm so sorry I didn't have the time."

"So am I." His eyes were sad. "There's a hole in the world."

"And in your heart," she added. She sat down in his lap and hugged him. "Time will help it heal."

He held her close, burying his face in her throat. "Yes."

"Are you sad, Daddy?" Markie asked, coming up on one side. "It's because my grandma died, isn't it?"

"Yes." Jon smiled at him. "It hurts."

"She was mean at first, but then she bought us ice cream." He sighed. "Now I won't have a grandma anymore."

"She would have spoiled him rotten," Jon said when Markie had gone back to his drawing.

"Yes."

He shifted her on his lap with a sigh. "I wonder what Rick Marquez is up to?" he murmured.

"Why do you think he's up to something?"

"He won't let me see the police report on Cammy's death."

She blinked. "He won't?"

He eyed her. "You could get it."

"Now, those are protected files behind firewalls," she began.

"And you can hack anything."

She pursed her lips. His eyes were twinkling. "Most anything," she agreed.

"Will you?"

"If you'll bring Markie to visit me in prison," she said under her breath, tongue-in-cheek.

"I'll get you the best criminal lawyer in San Antonio," he promised.

She got up. "Okay. I'll use a false identity and cross my fingers." She went to the computer on the dining room table and sat down to turn on the power.

Ten minutes later, she went back to Jon, frowning.

"What's wrong?" he asked.

"There are no files."

He blinked. "What?"

"No files at all. No photos, no evidence forms, nothing."

"That's not possible," he said curtly. "It's a murder case."

"I know. But nothing has been filed."

He was thinking, working in his mind. "It's only been a few days," he rationalized. "Perhaps they haven't had time to upload photos or other evidence."

She didn't answer him.

He took out his cell phone and called his brother. "Mac," he said. "There are no files on Cammy's murder."

"Have you led Joceline into a life of cybercrime trying to hack protected police files?" came the reply.

"Yes."

"No files, you say."

"Exactly."

"I'll dig around and let you know what I find." He hung up.

"Mac's going to try," he told Joceline. "This is confusing."

Joceline was chewing on the facts herself. Kilraven hadn't been allowed into the hotel room where Cammy died. There had been two strange men at the funeral home, and Jon said the funeral director had been disconcerted when they mentioned an open casket at the service. Now there were no files on the case. She added up those facts and produced a conclusion that she didn't dare voice.

Jon had reached the same conclusion. They looked at each other without speaking.

"There would have been no reason to stage it," she said for both of them.

"Unless they had knowledge of a plot to kill her and set it up to save her," he replied. "Maybe to get evidence that could be used against the would-be shooter and give them time to do more checking."

"Exactly."

His heart lifted suddenly. It might not be the tragedy he'd expected. Cammy might still be alive, in hiding, and Marquez had forbidden any knowledge of it to Jon or Joceline because he suspected someone working with them, someone who might accidentally find out that it was a setup.

Joceline gripped Jon's hand tight. "We could be wrong," she said. "There are plenty of circumstantial things that we're concocting into a theory."

"I know that."

"Is my apartment bugged, you think?" she wondered.

"If it is, we both know who bugged it," he replied. "And the killer can't have planted any listening devices here. They'd have been removed."

Jon's cell phone rang. He answered it.

"Yes, it's bugged, yes, someone did plant listening devices but I found them all," a deep voice with a curt South African accent replied. There was a chuckle. "Your conclusions are very interesting, but I'll say nothing to affirm or deny their correctness. You'll have to sit back and wait for results, like the rest of us."

"Where is Sloane Callum?" Jon asked.

"In a safe place. He put his own life on the line to help us with a project."

"There's a very dangerous person out there," Jon said quietly.

"You have no idea," Rourke replied tersely. "We've made some disturbing discoveries. I can't say any more."

"You've got somebody watching my brother and his wife?"

"Yes, also you and Joceline and the boy."

"All right. But I'd remind you that I do work for the premier law enforcement agency in the country."

315

"Which would get you carte blanche in this investigation except that you have one or more suspects in your very own office."

"One or more?" Jon burst out.

"I can't say any more. And don't try to pump Marquez," he added. "I trained him in counterespionage myself. He's incorruptible."

"Damn," Jon muttered.

"You'll like the result. Be patient."

Jon sighed. "Very well. Thanks, Rourke."

"Some odd things may happen tomorrow," Rourke added quietly. "Be on your guard, don't go anywhere alone. Make sure Joceline doesn't leave the building without you."

"What about my son?" Jon asked.

"We have two agents at the school," he replied. "He'll be safe. I give you my word, and I don't give it lightly."

"He'd better be."

"One other thing," he added.

"Yes?"

There was a pause. Jon heard someone else speaking, in a taut, firm tone. Rourke came back on the line. "I can't say anything else. Trust me. I have your best interests at heart."

"Didn't Napoleon make such a statement just before Waterloo?" Jon wondered aloud.

"That's your brother's thing, military history, not yours," he was reminded tongue-in-cheek. "Get a good night's sleep. You're going to need it." He hung up.

Jon looked at Joceline and then at his son with real worry. He didn't know what or how much to tell Joceline. He only hoped whoever was orchestrating this developing plot knew what they were doing. He wished he knew what it was.

14

The next day, Joceline sat at her desk, typing up reports on the computer, with her mind totally not on what she was doing. She was upset because of a hint Jon had given her about today. He'd said to be on her toes, and nothing more. She wondered what he meant. He was unusually protective, and tense, as if he was expecting danger.

Their part-time worker, Phyllis Hicks, had shown up for work, mingling with the other office workers on their floor. Joceline tried not to pay too much attention to her, but she was nervous. The woman had a look in her eyes, on her face, that was disconcerting. She didn't seem quite normal. Especially today.

Joceline averted her gaze to her work and tried not to notice that Phyllis was staring at her pointedly. But when the woman stopped beside her desk, she was forced to look up and smile, as if she knew nothing of the woman's background.

"Hi, Phyllis, how's school going?" she asked.

Phyllis raised an eyebrow. "You have a reputation in the office for being able to get information that nobody else can find," she said, lowering her voice. "So it's a safe bet that you've checked me out and found something that all the agents who investigated my background missed. I thought I'd covered it up very well," she added with a cold smile. "But I must have missed one little link somewhere."

"Excuse me?" Joceline said carelessly and with a feigned vacant smile.

"You know who my real father is."

"I do?" She smiled again.

"Stop it," Phyllis said, and her eyes took on an odd, feral sort of gleam. "No more games. They've been watching me, Marquez and his friends. My dad told me. He tells me everything. All I have to do is flatter him and make a fuss over him, and he'll dig into files for me. I say it's helping me to learn my job. He buys it, every time."

"He does?"

Phyllis placed her hands on the desk and leaned forward, so that her voice didn't carry. "My dad says they've got a file on me. It shocked him. He thinks they're trying to railroad me on an attempted murder charge, because I told him it was all lies. He was shocked that a good detective like Marquez would target a sweet, helpless little thing like me."

"Are cobras helpless?" Joceline asked.

"They'll never get enough evidence to convict me," she whispered. She smiled and seemed proud of herself, in a sick way. She started talking quickly, as if she couldn't stop. "I persuaded my real daddy into letting me go with him, to make sure Dan Jones did the job on Kilraven's daughter. I was just seventeen, but I was already a dead shot. My daddy taught me. Dan Jones was such a wimp. He couldn't shoot a child. He even cried. I took the shotgun away and killed the little girl with it. It was easy. Really easy. It didn't bother me at all. My daddy said I was a natural." Her eyes gleamed with an insane light while Joceline tried not to gag. "So he talked Jay Copper into letting me do some wet work for them. I could get in places they couldn't. My stepdad knew all sorts of things I could use, and he didn't have a clue he was feeding me information I gave to my real dad. I could even get weapons out of the evidence room and put them back, nobody ever suspected me.

Imagine, hiding a murder weapon in an evidence room." She laughed. Her face clenched. "Then that stupid Monroe had to go and claim credit for my kill, mine! He blabbed about the shotgun. I should never have told my real daddy where I put it. You can't tell people anything these days. Nobody can keep his mouth shut!"

"You killed a child," Joceline said, horrified.

"What's one less kid in the world?" she asked blankly. "I was going to do yours, but they wouldn't let me. They said killing his secretary's kid wouldn't hurt him nearly as much as doing his mother." She laughed again, coldly. "So I found out where she was staying, listening in on her conversations with her son, and I took a wheel gun with the serial number filed off and did her, right in her hotel room, while she was on the phone with Kilraven." She laughed harder. "That was so funny. Imagine how he felt when he heard her die and couldn't do a thing!"

Joceline's mouth was half open. The woman was confessing to two murders, in an FBI office, to Joceline and she wasn't wired and the office wasn't bugged. It would be hearsay evidence, no matter what oaths Joceline swore to tell the truth.

"You really are out of your mind," Joceline said tautly.

"Don't say that!" she snapped at the older woman. "They said that about my grandmother because she killed herself. My real daddy told her what I did. She couldn't take it. She overdosed on some pills." She straightened. "She was really weak. But I'm strong. I can do anything, just like my real daddy. He killed Dan Jones. He wouldn't let me go with him that time, but he told me all about it. It was so exciting!" she whispered, her eyes gleaming. "He said Jones cried and begged him and Jay Copper not to kill him. The idiot got religion. He was going to sell out Jay Copper and my real daddy. Well, they got Copper, but they didn't get my daddy and they won't get me, either. And Harold Monroe is going to die. He isn't part of our family anyway — he's just married to my aunt!"

"You can't think they won't find evidence to convict you," Joceline said quietly. "You won't get away with it."

"Who's going to arrest me?" she chided. "And on what evidence — your word? Kilraven and his new wife told them they heard Jay Copper say that my daddy helped him kill that girl, but once the tape was gone, they couldn't prosecute daddy. It was just their word against his."

"How did that tape disappear?"

"I took it out of the evidence room." She smirked. "And we had a friend get in your apartment and take the records that proved I was daddy's illegitimate daughter," she added coldly. "I took the files out of the mainframe computer, here. It's handy, working for the FBI," she added.

"You can't think you'll get away with it," Joceline said.

"Why not?" the other woman asked with a careless laugh. "I've never even been under suspicion." Her eyes narrowed. "Your kid's been lucky so far. Hasn't he?"

Joceline got to her feet. Her blue eyes were glittering as she moved toward the other woman. "If you touch my son, if you even think of touching him, you won't be able to hide anywhere on earth."

"You think you could stop me?" Phyllis replied.

"I think someone has to," Joceline said quietly, "before you hurt someone else's child. You're absolutely insane."

"Don't . . . say . . . that!" Phyllis lunged at her, lightning-fast, pushing her back across the desk. "I'm not crazy!" She had her hands around Joceline's throat, her nails biting in, and Joceline could hardly breathe. If they didn't hurry . . . !

"And that's enough of that, lady." A gruff voice came from over Phyllis's shoulder. She was pulled upright, turned around and handcuffed in a fluid, easy motion.

"What the hell . . . ?" Phyllis exclaimed.

Joceline got to her feet, a little shaky. Jon put his arm around her, examined her throat and grimaced. She only smiled at him, safe and relieved.

"It may take us a little time to wrap up all the loose ends," Detective Marquez told the furious, red-faced killer, "but we get there." He motioned to the two uniformed officers he'd brought with him, one of whom had Phyllis by the arm. "And notice that I'm reading you your rights. I wouldn't want to leave one single loophole for a defense attorney." He read her the Miranda rights.

"You set me up!" Phyllis exclaimed, glaring furiously at a shell-shocked Joceline.

"Actually Rourke set you up," Jon said coldly, "with a little help from Detectives Marquez here, and Gail Rogers. This time the tapes won't go missing, I promise you. Your stepfather is down at police headquarters trying to explain how he helped you get into the evidence room."

"He won't tell them anything!" she spat.

"Oh, he's up for retirement in six months.

I expect he'll tell them whatever they want to know," Jon added. His eyes were cold as ice. "You killed my niece, and my mother. I'll be at every parole hearing until I die. You'll never get out of prison."

"First they have to convict me," she said sweetly, "and they have no evidence."

Jon gave her a quiet stare. "I suppose it didn't occur to you that shotgun shells need to be wiped of prints as well as the barrel of the gun?"

She stared back at him blankly, and then with dawning realization. "Monroe!" she burst out. "That stupid, stupid idiot told them where the murder weapon was hidden!"

"He took the blame for it," Jon lied, "to save you."

She shifted, surprised. "He doesn't even like me."

"You're part of his family, aren't you?" he asked, and surprised himself defending Monroe.

"I guess so." She sighed angrily. "But the idiot put a noose around my neck all the same. My real daddy will take care of him!"

"Oh, I don't think so," Kilraven said, joining them. He smiled coldly at the woman who'd killed his three-year-old daughter. He had to fight the instinct that was telling

325

him to snap her neck before she could even get to jail. "Your real daddy has been arrested and charged with complicity in the murder of my wife and child. You see, there were two sets of fingerprints on those shotgun shells." He didn't add that they wouldn't be able to identify those prints officially until she was arrested and booked and fingerprinted. He was hedging his bets.

She was absolutely at a loss for words. Her face went red, and not from embarrassment. She let out a barrage of curses, some of which had Jon lifting his eyebrows.

"Get her out of here," Jon advised the policemen. He was still afraid that Kilraven might do something regrettable.

"Good idea," Kilraven said icily.

They removed her. Kilraven, Jon and Joceline watched her go with the same expressions.

"What a shock," Jon said heavily.

Detective Marquez came closer, his hands in his pockets. He grimaced. "I'm afraid the shocks aren't over for the day."

"What?" Jon asked hesitantly.

"You have to promise not to hit me," he told the brothers. "It was the only thing I could think of to save her, especially after your employee Sloane Callum phoned me, all upset, and told me that he'd heard what

326

was going down once Cammy Blackhawk got to the hotel. I got an earful about Jay Copper's family tree in the process. So I came up with this idea, to let the killer think she'd scored a direct hit. I had no idea that Rourke had some knowledge of Hollywood-style special effects," he added thoughtfully.

"Special effects?" Jon asked.

Marquez shifted. "Sorry, I was thinking out loud about the guy's background. Yes. Sloane called Monroe and had him pay Phyllis a visit. He knew what sort of gun she carried. While she was out of the room, he switched clips. She fired blanks from a concealed position and thanks to some carefully rigged explosive charges over a Kevlar vest, it looked as if real bullets had caused major damage to Cammy's chest. Phyllis left without checking closer, thank God. It would have ruined the setup and we'd have blown the case."

"Wait a minute," Jon faltered. "Cammy's not dead?"

"She's alive?" Kilraven echoed, dumbfounded.

"Alive and still cursing me for putting the two of you through a mock murder." Marquez sighed. "My medical insurance is paid up, so if you want to punch me . . . !"

Both brothers grabbed him at the same

time and hugged him, even Jon, who was notorious for avoiding displays of public affection.

Joceline laughed, delighted. "What a trick! No wonder you wouldn't let Kilraven or Alice Fowler into the crime scene or give them access to the police report on the 'murder'!"

Marquez glared at her. "Yes, despite your best efforts to hack my computer."

"Oooops!" she said, red-faced.

"About which, fortunately for you, I know nothing," he added.

"Thank goodness!" she said. "I look terrible in orange jumpsuits!"

"Where is she?" Jon asked.

"At the ranch," he replied, chuckling at their surprise. "Sloane said it was the safest place, because he'd kill anything that came near her. He was indignant that a cousin of his was responsible for this mess, even if she was only related to his son by marriage."

"Harold Monroe is his son," Jon reminded Marquez.

"I know. I wired his inmate-friend to record his so-called confession." He laughed. "This has been one incredible case. In all my years with the force, I've never come across anything similar. Well, except for this one case, in my days as a police officer, when a state senator's wife was involved

328

in a grisly murder and went to prison for it. Judd Dunn was involved in that one. So was Cash Grier."

"I remember. The senator was Dunn's best friend. Tragic case. Didn't the senator marry his secretary?" Kilraven asked.

"Yes, they have two little boys now. He's retired from politics and spends his time pushing legislation to help farmers."

"Happy endings."

"Very. I want to see Cammy," Jon said.

"Me, too," his brother seconded.

"We'll all go," Joceline said. "Can you go ask the SAC if we can have the rest of the day off?" she asked Jon.

He grinned. "On my way."

"I'll get back to work before the shock and relief wear off and they start looking for blunt instruments of violence," Marquez mused, glancing from one brother to the other.

"We wouldn't hit you," Jon protested.

"Well, we wouldn't hit you hard," Kilraven amended. And he grinned.

Cammy was waiting at the front door when the five of them arrived. She grabbed her sons and hugged and hugged them and cried and hugged them some more. They were doing much the same.

Eventually she let them go and embraced Joceline and Winnie and bent to pick up little Markie, who was unsettled by all the emotion.

"It's okay," Joceline told her son, "these are happy tears. We thought your grandmother was . . . well, that we wouldn't see her again."

"I know. There was a funeral and I couldn't go." He looked at his grandmother and touched her silver-threaded black hair in its high, elegant bun. "I'm so glad you didn't die, Granny."

Her eyes teared up again and she hugged him closer. "Me, too. Oh, I'm so happy!"

"So are we," Winnie murmured, and she hugged Cammy, as well.

A few days later, they sat around the huge, open fireplace in the living room and talked over the shattering events of the past months.

Sloane Callum started into the room, his cowboy hat gripped in one big hand, but he hesitated when he saw all the people.

Jon got up and went to him, his eyes black and quiet as they met the other man's.

"I know, I'm fired," Callum said heavily. "I should have told you about my own son, and my family connections, long ago. But I

330

thought you wouldn't want to trust me . . ."

Jon hugged him, hard. "You saved Cammy's life. And because we hired you, your son helped us find the killer of my niece, Melly, and Mac's first wife." He took the other man by the shoulders. "Don't even think about quitting. We owe you."

"All of us," Kilraven agreed quietly.

"Especially me," Cammy added, and smiled at Callum. "I knew you'd be a wonderful addition to the ranch staff. I was right." She looked at her sons and glared. "I'm always right, so you should listen to me when I tell you things for your own good."

"You wanted me to marry Charlene," Jon reminded her.

"And you wanted me to stop seeing Winnie," Kilraven reminded her.

She threw up her hands. "Two little mistakes!" She sighed.

They laughed.

"I will try to reform," she said in a gentle tone. "From now on, I'm going to keep out of your business and mind my own." She sat down beside Joceline. "There are just one or two things. Small things. You should take Markie to a lung specialist and let them do tests, and I'll pay for it. You should have a pretty wedding gown. We can go to Neiman Marcus and pick one out. And we should do something about the color scheme in Jon's apartment — there should be bright colors . . ."

Jon and Kilraven got up. "We're going to buy Callum a beer," they said, then spoiled their exit by bursting into laughter just outside the living room door.

"Now what in the world are they laughing at?" Cammy wondered aloud. "Never mind, about Jon's apartment . . ." she continued, unabashed.

Joceline and Winnie exchanged amused glances, but they paid rapt attention.

EPILOGUE

Phyllis Hicks was charged with the murder of Kilraven's first wife and his daughter, as well as the attempted murder of Cammy Blackhawk, and many other charges. She would be put away for a long time, and there would be no other children who would be hurt by her madness.

The murder charges against Harold Monroe were quietly dropped. He vanished out of sight, amidst rumors that he was in some sort of federal protection program. They were only rumors, of course.

Jon and Joceline were married in the interdenominational church in San Antonio that Joceline had attended for years, with flower girls and Markie as ring bearer, and Winnie and Cammy as dual matrons of honor. Many of the San Antonio FBI agents found a way to attend, though some had to watch the ceremony on a DVD later.

Joceline and Markie moved in with Jon,

but she kept her job at the office. Cammy argued that she should stay home with Markie, but Jon argued that he'd go nuts if he had to break in a new assistant. He won, too.

Markie's behavior improved to such a degree that any decisions about medication were left for future discussion, perhaps the result of a much more settled home life.

Winnie Kilraven was rushed to the hospital with labor pains just a week before Christmas. She produced a tiny little boy with a thick head of black hair, and big tough McKuen Kilraven cried as he held his son in his arms.

Jon and Joceline put up a Christmas tree in his apartment with ornaments that had been handed down for generations in his family, and some of the small ones she and Markie had accumulated from Christmases past in her apartment. Cammy had contributed a beautiful Swarovski crystal one for their first Christmas together as a family. She and the Kilravens were going to join Jon and Joceline and Markie at the ranch for the yearly mealfest. Joceline was looking forward to it. So was Markie. In view of the near-tragedies, it was going to be a marvelous celebration of life.

The tree was tall and round and tapered

and beautiful. Markie just stared at it in awe when Joceline brought him home from day care to find it already set up with the lights blaring in the living room.

"Oh, it's like magic!" he exclaimed, touching it almost reverently.

Jon's arm went around Joceline and pulled her close. He looked down into her soft, loving eyes with absolute wonder. "Yes. It is like magic."

"Daddy, do you love Mommy?" Markie asked him suddenly, looking up at him with big, wide blue eyes.

Joceline was embarrassed. Jon had never said the words, not even when he was the most passionate. "Markie," she began, in protest.

Jon cupped Joceline's face in his big, warm hands. "I love her more than anything or anyone in the world," he said softly, and smiled at her surprise as he bent to kiss her with breathless tenderness.

"More than you love me?" Markie asked plaintively.

Jon chuckled. He picked the boy up in his arms and kissed his hair. "I love both of you more than anything in the world," he amended.

"I love you, too, Daddy." Markie sighed, and hugged the tall man warmly. "I was just thinking," he added thoughtfully. "Wouldn't it be nice if I had a brother like you do?"

Jon looked at Joceline with a wicked smile. "Wouldn't it?" he mused.

Joceline laughed and colored prettily. They hadn't used precautions at all, so much in love that the addition of a child to the family would be a wonder, not a worry. In fact, she was already late on her monthly.

Jon knew. His eyes twinkled.

"Or a sister, I guess," Markie told them. "I could teach her how to draw."

"Truly," Joceline agreed.

Markie looked past them at the majestic Christmas tree. "It's going to be the best Christmas we ever had, Mommy!" he burst out.

She looked at her husband and her child, and her blue eyes were overflowing with joy. "Yes, my darling," she told him. "The best Christmas ever!"

ABOUT THE AUTHOR

The prolific author of over 100 books, **Diana Palmer** got her start as a newspaper reporter. A multi-*New York Times* bestselling author and one of the top ten romance writers in America, she has a gift for telling the most sensual tales with charm and humor. Diana lives with her family in Cornelia, Georgia.

The employees of Thorndike Press hope you have enjoyed this Large Print book. All our Thorndike, Wheeler, and Kennebec Large Print titles are designed for easy reading, and all our books are made to last. Other Thorndike Press Large Print books are available at your library, through selected bookstores, or directly from us.

For information about titles, please call:
(800) 223-1244

or visit our Web site at:
http://gale.cengage.com/thorndike

To share your comments, please write:
Publisher
Thorndike Press
10 Water St., Suite 310
Waterville, ME 04901